★ ★ ★ WHAT'S ON ★ ★ ★
SPELLOVISION

6.00 Zombie Decorating
The Zombies paint a room – and watch it dry.

7.00 The News with *Sheridan Haggard*
The Skeleton with the Golden Voice brings you all the
Witchway news.
*Followed by the weather, presented by our glamorous
Zombie weather girl, Brenda.*

7.30 Gnome and Away
GNarleen's in love with GNorman, who's secretly going
out with GNometta, who's got a secret crush on
GNeville . . .
Repeated tomorrow at 12 noon

8.00 Familiar Fortunes
Tonight the Toad family try for the big prizes.

9.00 Goblins in Cars
Those crazy Mountain Goblins are racing more beat-up
old cars. No rules, no skills, just lots of crashes.
Repeated Friday at 10.30pm

10.00 Fiends

Six Fiends sit and drink coffee and talk about each other's
problems.
See Pick of the Week: page 24

DON'T FORGET – TOMORROW NIGHT
THE GREAT SPELLOVISION
SONG CONTEST!
★ ★ ★ ★ ★ ★ ★ ★ ★ ★ ★

Kaye Umansky was born in Plymouth, Devon. Her favourite books as a child were the *Just William* books, *Alice's Adventures in Wonderland*, *The Hobbit* and *The Swish of the Curtain*. She went to teachers' training college, and then she taught in London primary schools for twelve years, specializing in music and drama. In her spare time she sang and played keyboards with a semi-professional soul band.

She now writes full time – or as full time as she can in between trips to Sainsbury's and looking after her husband (Mo), daughter (Ella) and cats (Tilly and Charlie).

Other books by Kaye Umansky

PONGWIFFY
PONGWIFFY AND THE GOBLINS' REVENGE
PONGWIFFY AND THE SPELL OF THE YEAR
PONGWIFFY AND THE HOLIDAY OF DOOM
PONGWIFFY AND THE PANTOMIME

WILMA'S WICKED REVENGE
WILMA'S WICKED SPELL

THE FWOG PWINCE: THE TWUTH!

PRINCE DANDYPANTS AND THE MASKED AVENGER

For younger readers

THE DRESSED-UP GIANT
GOBLINZ!

PONGWIFFY

THE SPELLOVISION SONG CONTEST

KAYE UMANSKY

Illustrated by David Roberts

PUFFIN BOOKS

PUFFIN BOOKS

Published by the Penguin Group
Penguin Books Ltd, 80 Strand, London WC2R 0RL, England
Penguin Putnam Inc., 375 Hudson Street, New York, New York 10014, USA
Penguin Books Australia Ltd, 250 Camberwell Road, Camberwell, Victoria 3124, Australia
Penguin Books Canada Ltd, 10 Alcorn Avenue, Toronto, Ontario, Canada M4V 3B2
Penguin Books India (P) Ltd, 11 Community Centre, Panchsheel Park, New Delhi – 110 017, India
Penguin Books (NZ) Ltd, Cnr Rosedale and Airborne Roads, Albany, Auckland, New Zealand
Penguin Books (South Africa) (Pty) Ltd, 24 Sturdee Avenue, Rosebank 2196, South Africa

Penguin Books Ltd, Registered Offices: 80 Strand, London WC2R 0RL, England

www.penguin.com

First published 2003
1

Set in Bembo

Made and printed in England by Clays Ltd, St Ives plc

British Library Cataloguing in Publication Data A CIP catalogue record for this book is available
from the British Library

ISBN 0–141–31014–6

To Mo and Ella

CONTENTS

Get your entry forms
NOW for the

SPELLOVISION
SONG CONTEST

☆

Songs must be original

☆

Fabulous prizes to be won!

☆

Anyone can enter — EXCEPT GOBLINS

CHAPTER ONE
A Visit to Sharkadder

'Moon's up. I think I'll go out,' announced Witch Pongwiffy to Hugo, her Hamster Familiar.

'OK,' said Hugo, not even looking up. He was comfortably curled up in the tea cosy, nose deep in a very small book. A saucer full of chopped carrot was within easy reach. The kettle was boiling, ready to pour into a thimble of cocoa.

'You coming?' asked Pongwiffy, taking her hat from its hook.

'No. I is readink.'

'Who said you could read? You're supposed to be working for me, not reading. What is it, anyway? A book of stamps? Hm? Little sticky stamps? Is that why you've had your nose stuck in it for days?'

'No. Is *Ze Little Book of Hamster Vit and Visdom*. Is collection of clever Hamster sayinks.'

'Oh yeah? No wonder it's small. OK, OK, only joking. Tell me one.'

'*Hamsters might be small, but zey haf great big hearts*,' Hugo read out.

'Rubbish!' said Pongwiffy. 'If your hearts were big, there wouldn't be room for the rest of the stuff. Your tummy and lungs and daft little kidneys. What else?'

'*Hamsters are better zan cats.*'

'Hamsters are better than cats?' scoffed Pongwiffy. 'What kind of saying is that? That's not wise or witty.'

'Is true though,' said Hugo firmly.

'Why? How are they better?'

'In every vay. Hamsters better lookink, tougher, got better personality. See zis scar?' Hugo pointed to his ear. 'A cat did zat. Boy, voz he sorry.' He turned a page of his book and gave a little snigger. 'Listen. Zis good vun. *If ignorance is bliss, vy are cats so miserable?*'

'Hm,' said Pongwiffy. 'Is there a *lot* of anti-cat stuff in the book?'

'Loads,' said Hugo. 'Vant to hear more?'

'No. I'm bored with cats.'

'How about zis, zen? *Blue are ze violets, red are ze roses. Hamsters are furry, viz little pink noses.*'

'Good grief! Is that the best you lot can come up with?' said Pongwiffy, unimpressed. 'I'm off. Perhaps I'll take the Broom and fly over to Sharkadder's.'

The Broom, which had been quivering hopefully in a dark corner, came flying out and started attacking the door enthusiastically.

'OK,' said Hugo, head back in his book. 'Bye, zen.'

'Sure you won't come?'

'Huh? Oh. No. Zis is gripping stuff.'

'About as gripping as the elastic on my oldest pair of knickers,' sneered Pongwiffy. Which was a rude thing to say, but we'll forgive her because she was disappointed that Hugo wasn't coming.

Out she went, with the Broom whizzing eagerly round her in little circles, keen to be up and away.

Pongwiffy's hovel – Number One, Dump Edge – stood on the edge of a huge rubbish tip. The beauty of it was that the view from her window was constantly changing. There was the rusty cooker and the broken mangle and the three-legged pram and the pile of mouldering old mattresses, of course. They'd been there for years. But every week, fresh junk magically appeared, adding fascinating new smells and textures. As Pongwiffy was always boasting to anyone who would listen, she never got bored.

3

She stood in her doorway, closed her eyes, and breathed in the familiar smell of rotting garbage. Tonight, it had subtle new overtones. There had obviously been a new delivery. Should she go and pick over it now, or save that pleasure for later?

Her mind was made up by the Broom (Woody), which had been cooped up too long and was now fly-crazy. It kept jumping up at her in an annoying, puppyish way, then nipping round and banging into the back of her knees, trying to get her to climb on.

'All right,' she said. 'Stop your nonsense, we're going, we're going.'

Seconds later, they were airborne. They skimmed over the trees, enjoying the cool night breeze. Below lay Witchway Wood – dark, silent and strangely empty.

'Seems quiet down there tonight,' shouted Pongwiffy over the wind. 'No smoke from the chimneys. Looks like everyone's out. Hey! It's not the last Friday of the month, is it? I'm not missing a Coven meeting, am I?'

The Broom didn't reply. It could only speak in Wood. Besides, it wasn't the brightest Broom in the cupboard. It *never* knew what day it was.

'Actually, it's Tuesday,' mused Pongwiffy. 'I remember now, because yesterday was Monday, when I always water the toadstools under my pillow. Strange how quiet everything is, though ...'

Witch Sharkadder stood on her doorstep, locking up. She was dressed up to the nines – hair a mass of tortured curls, spider-leg eyelashes, lipstick (Mad Mildew), perfume (Oppression, French, very posh), freshly sharpened nails, the works. Her Familiar, a one-eyed cat called Deadeye Dudley, was glaring sullenly out of the window, clearly put out at being left behind. Her Broom, name of Ashley, was propped against the drainpipe. A green ribbon was tied in a floppy bow around its stick.

Everyone winced as Pongwiffy came hurtling down into the flowerbed, boots ploughing up the neat row of delicate crocuses that had just begun to show their shy little heads.

'Oh,' said Sharkadder with a little sigh. 'It's you, Pong. What a pity, I'm just off out.'

'Lucky I caught you, then,' said Pongwiffy, climbing off her Broom, which took one look at Ashley's ribbon and fell about laughing. (To your ear and mine, this would sound like straightforward rustling.)

'But I'm going out,' repeated Sharkadder, popping her key in her handbag.

'That's all right. I'll come with you. Where are you going, anyway?'

'Visiting.'

'Well, I can see that. Who?'

'Oh – just a friend,' hedged Sharkadder, snapping the bag shut. 'I can't stay here talking to you all night, I'm late as it is.'

'What friend?' persisted Pongwiffy. 'A better friend than me?'

'No, of course not. You're my best friend, you know that.'

'Who, then?'

'Nobody special.'

'*Who?*'

'Well – Sourmuddle, if you must know.'

'Oh *really*? Nobody *special,* eh?' Pongwiffy sneered. Sourmuddle was only the Grandwitch, boss of the Witchway Coven. She was certainly special.

'She's having a sort of small, select gathering,' mumbled Sharkadder, going a bit pink.

'*Really?*' Pongwiffy's eyebrows shot up in surprise. Sourmuddle wasn't known for her hospitality. She usually took her meals at other Witches' cottages. It was one of the advantages of rank. 'Like who?'

'Well – me. And I think Macabre will be there.'

'Is that all?'

'Well – the twins. And Ratsnappy.'

'Anyone else?'

'Greymatter. Oh, and Gaga.'

'What about Sludgegooey and Scrofula?'

'Um ... yes. I believe so.' Sharkadder had reached the carefully-looking-the-other-way stage.

'And Bonidle and Bendyshanks?' enquired Pongwiffy sternly.

Sharkadder looked down and twiddled her high-heeled shoe.

'Probably.'

'That's not a small, select gathering,' Pongwiffy pointed out. 'That's the whole Coven!'

'Erm – yes.'

'Everyone except me!'

'Erm – yes.'

'Well, that's just terrific!' sulked Pongwiffy. 'I was wondering where everyone was. And now I know. There's a thundering great party at Sourmuddle's and I'm not invited!'

'It's not exactly a *party*.'

'What, then?'

'Oh, all right, if you must know. Sourmuddle's got one of those new spellovisions and we're all going round to watch it. It's not that she doesn't *want* you, Pong. But you know how small her parlour is and, quite frankly, your smell in an enclosed space is ...'

'Never mind my smell. Go back a bit. She's got a *what*?'

'A spellovision.'

'And what's that, when it's at home?'

'Surely you must have heard of *spellovision*!' Sharkadder pretended to be amazed, although, in fact, she had only just heard about it herself. 'It's *quite* the new thing. It's a sort of square box and you sit and watch it.'

'What's the point of sitting and watching a box?' asked Pongwiffy. 'I've got a box at home. I keep coal in it, along with my spare socks. I've never felt the need to sit and watch it, though.'

'No, no. This is different. It's – a new sort of Magic. Invisible pictures come through the air and get caught in the box. Sourmuddle says it's got a screen. You twiddle knobs and the pictures come alive and you watch them.'

'What are the pictures of?'

'I don't know, do I? That's why I'm going to Sourmuddle's to find out.'

'Well!' said Pongwiffy, highly miffed. 'I think I'll just come along too. I don't see why I should be left out.'

'Oh, don't go all huffy. If it's any consolation, the Familiars aren't allowed to come. No room, see. So you're not the only one.'

'That's different. I'm a Witch. It's discrimination, that's what it is, and I shall say so in no uncertain terms. In fact, I shall give Sourmuddle a piece of my mind.'

'Suit yourself,' said Sharkadder with a shrug. 'But don't bring me into it.'

CHAPTER TWO
Watching Spellovision

'...so I called in on Sharkadder and she mentioned she was about to come over to you and I was wondering if I could come in and watch your spellovision, please?' begged Pongwiffy humbly. It was easy to *talk* about giving Sourmuddle a piece of her mind, but a bit different when she was there in the flesh, glaring on the doorstep.

'Don't blame me,' said Sharkadder disloyally. '*I* didn't ask her.'

Sourmuddle peered over the top of her glasses.

'It's very crowded in the parlour,' she said.

'I'll make myself small.'

'It's stuffy too. I'm not sure I can accommodate you.'

'It's my smell, isn't it? My smell's not welcome. All right. Just this once, I'll squirt myself with Sharkadder's perfume.'

'What, at ten pounds a bottle? Not likely,' said Sharkadder unhelpfully.

'Then I'll sit by the window.'

'There aren't enough peanuts,' said Sourmuddle.

'I don't mind. I'm not hungry. Look. I'm getting on my knees and begging.' Pongwiffy sank to her knees and wrung her hands in supplication. 'Please! O pretty please! Pleasepleasepleasepleasepleasepleasepleasepleaseplea–'

'All right,' said Sourmuddle grudgingly. 'But you'll have to keep quiet. This is a momentous occasion and I'm not having you spoiling it.'

'I'll be good,' promised Pongwiffy, which was rather like a monkey promising not to eat bananas.

The parlour was hot and crowded. Every available seat was taken, apart from the rocking chair, which was reserved for Sourmuddle. Witches Macabre, Greymatter and Agglebag and Bagaggle, the twins, were squashed on the sofa. Bonidle snoozed in an armchair, flanked by Ratsnappy and Sludgegooey, who perched on the arms. Bendyshanks and Scrofula sat on upright chairs that had been brought in from the kitchen. Gaga hung from the curtain rail, because she preferred dangling to sitting.

They all faced a large, mysterious, square box with a grey screen, which sat in pride of place on Sourmuddle's best coffee table.

'Oh,' said Bendyshanks, rising hastily. 'It's Pongwiffy. I'll open the window.'

Agglebag and Macabre squeezed up even more to make room for Sharkadder, and Pongwiffy picked her way over to the open window and stood obediently in the draught.

Out in the starry garden, she noticed, Woody had pulled off Ashley's ribbon and was waving it around in a confrontational sort of way.

'Right,' said Sourmuddle, coming in from the kitchen with a very small bowl. 'Nuts first. Pass them round, would you, Ratsnappy? I think you'll find there's exactly one each. Except for Pongwiffy, who wasn't invited.'

The bowl was passed round and everyone except Pongwiffy carefully took a nut. There was a lot of exaggerated lip smacking and smarmy cries of 'Delicious!' and 'My, that hit the spot!' Buttering up Sourmuddle was in everyone's interest.

'Good,' said Sourmuddle. 'Never let it be said that I'm mean with the catering.' She walked over to the square box and put her hand on one of the knobs.

'Well, you all know why you're here. I've got one of these newfangled spellovision sets. Only for research, you understand. As Grandwitch, it's my responsibility to keep up with any new fad that comes along. Anyway, it's the very latest thing and I thought you'd like to see what all the fuss is about. Remember, you saw it here first. Can everybody see?'

'Yes!' came the excited chorus. Pongwiffy couldn't, but thought she might be pushing her luck by saying so. Out in the garden, things were getting interesting. Ashley had got his ribbon back and was being chased round the water barrel by Woody.

'Ready?' said Sourmuddle. 'Here we go, then. Prepare to be amazed.'

She pressed the knob. A thrilled gasp went up as important-sounding music swelled and the screen flickered into life!

A smooth-looking Skeleton, wearing a smart bow tie, sat behind a desk with a pile of papers before him.

'Oooh!' gasped the watching Witches, craning forward excitedly. 'Look at that! Just like real life!'

'*Hello and welcome,*' said the Skeleton in a rich, golden-brown voice. '*I am Sheridan Haggard and you are watching the midnight news, brought to you from the Witchway news desk. Here are the main points. The*

Wizards have announced the date of their Annual Convention. It will take place on …'

'Move your hat, Greymatter, I can't see,' complained Pongwiffy.

'Sssssh!' hissed everybody.

'*… and will be staying as usual at the Magicians' Retreat, Sludgehaven-on-Sea. A Wizard was quoted as saying, "We like it there. The sausages are good."'*

'But I can't *see!*' insisted Pongwiffy, bobbing around, attempting to find a gap in the forest of pointy hats.

'Once more and you're out!' snapped Sourmuddle.

Pongwiffy subsided.

'*Earlier today,*' continued Sheridan Haggard, '*a daring masked Troll attempted to rob a small Gnome of his lunch. Young GNelson Pondworthy was out fishing when the attack occurred. The Troll swallowed a cheese sandwich, a strawberry yoghurt and half a carrot before being bravely beaten off with a fishing rod by have-a-go GNelson. His mother, Mrs GNorma Pondworthy, said, "My boy is a hero."*

'*The Banshee jumble sale, held last week, raised a record nine pence. It will go towards topping up the tin of teabags, which is getting perilously low …*'

'Gnome muggings!' scoffed Pongwiffy. She just couldn't help it. 'Jumble sales! Wizard Conventions! Hah! As if anyone cares.'

Rather to her surprise, nobody said a word. They were all hunched forward, eyes glued to the screen, hanging on to the Skeleton's every golden-brown word.

Out in the garden, the Brooms had come to blows. Ashley had had enough and was attacking Woody with its stick. Woody was defending itself by trying to brush Ashley away. Other Brooms had gathered in a circle and were rustling wildly, egging the combatants on. It was quite exciting. Pongwiffy wished she was out there, cheering from the sidelines.

'*Sales of spellovision sets are rising hourly, due to unprecedented public demand,*' Sheridan Haggard announced. '*From tomorrow, the* Daily Miracle *will be printing details of forthcoming programmes in place of the usual crossword puzzle. Order your copies now to beat the rush. That is the end of the news. And now a word from our glamorous weather girl. Brenda, over to you.*'

The scene changed. A bored-looking female Zombie in a bright pink suit teamed with green hair and big brass earrings stood before a badly drawn map of Witchway Wood. She was chewing pink bubblegum and holding a fistful of cut-out cardboard clouds.

'*Oh. Is it me? Right. Yeah,*' said Brenda the

glamorous weather girl. She reached into her mouth, took out the gum and used it to stick the largest cut-out cloud slap bang in the middle of the map, where it obscured pretty well everything.

''S gonna rain,' she said. 'Proberly. As if I care.'

She vanished, and Sheridan Haggard filled the screen again.

'Thank you, Brenda. Well, that's it from me. Stay tuned for tonight's film, Gnome Alone, a comedy for all the family about a young Gnome who gets left alone only to find himself at the mercy of two wicked Brownies who . . .'

'Not more Gnomes,' complained Pongwiffy. She'd had enough Gnomes for one night. Her boredom threshold as far as Gnomes were concerned was very low. She was Gnomed out.

Night beckoned through the open window. To her disappointment, the Broom fight was over. The Brooms had lost interest and were wandering around sweeping up a few twigs and grass cuttings. Woody was currently bashing at the garden gate, desperate to be up and away. Ashley was licking its bristles over by the rain barrel. There was no sign of the green ribbon. Who had won or lost wasn't very clear.

In the parlour, nobody spoke. On the screen, to the accompaniment of jaunty music, a family of Gnomes were packing suitcases and throwing fishing rods into a cart, obviously off on a fishing trip. The dialogue went like this:

FATHER: *Let us go on a fishing trip.*
MOTHER: *Oh yes. It will be fun.*
TEENAGE BOY GNOME: *I will take my rod.*
TEENAGE GIRL GNOME: *We will catch some fish.*
ALL: *It will be good.*

Pongwiffy gave a loud, ostentatious yawn. She had been involved in quite a few theatrical ventures in her time. She knew a bad script when she heard one.

'Is it me,' she enquired, 'or does anyone else find the acting wooden? I mean, *look* at 'em. I've seen gateposts with more personality.'

Silence. It was very clear that everyone else found it enthralling.

'Hello? Anyone listening?'

No one was, apparently.

'No one's bored, then? Personally, I am. I'm bored stiff. There was a Broom fight outside just now, did anyone notice?'

More silence.

'Shall we turn it off now and have a cup of bogwater? I could tell you all about this new spell I've been working on. It's very easy. You take a bucket of coal and mix it with treacle, by hand. Then add ...'

'Shhhhh!' came the furious, hissed chorus. On screen, the Gnome family were in the fascinating process of locking up the house.

FATHER: *I have a key. I will lock up the house.*
MOTHER: *Yes. Then we will go on our holiday.*
TEENAGE GIRL GNOME: *It will be fun.*
TEENAGE BOY GNOME: *Yes. Let us go.*

Pongwiffy gave up. She slipped through the open window and left them to it. The Broom came bounding up to meet her. She straddled the stick and they took off and went on a nice long flight to Crag Hill and back, which they both enjoyed.

Hugo was still up reading when they got back.

'Hi. Haf good time? Vot you do?' he asked.

'I've been watching spellovision,' said Pongwiffy.

'Vot zat?'

'You haven't heard of *spellovision*? I thought everyone knew. It's a Magic box and you turn it on and watch rubbish.'

'Vot sort of rubbish?'

So Pongwiffy told him all about it.

'... and there are altogether too many Gnomes,' she finished. 'Nothing of interest for Witches. It's just another fad. I'm sure it won't catch on.'

CHAPTER THREE
Quite the New Thing

Spellovision did more than catch on. It took over. Before the week was out, almost everybody in the wood had a spellovision set. If you stood on Crag Hill and looked in the direction of Witchway, you would notice a cold, bluish glow in an empty sky through which no Broomsticks flew.

Nobody went out at night any more. Nobody went herb gathering or shopping. The Skeletons stopped having picnics. The Trolls stopped playing rockball. The woods were empty of all but the rabbits and foxes. As for the Witches – they were well and truly hooked. If a Witch went scurrying by, you could be sure that she'd be on her way home with a last-minute takeaway before slumping on the sofa and growing square eyes. Nobody cooked any more. Nobody did any spells or any housework. Wands lay abandoned in dark corners. Nobody even picked up a crystal ball to talk to a friend.

Pongwiffy went round to Sharkadder's to complain about it. They sat in the kitchen. Well, Pongwiffy sat. Sharkadder hovered by the door in a strange half-crouch, trying to conceal a large wooden crate that had arrived that morning and which she hadn't yet had time to unpack. Dudley sat glaring down from the top of the dresser, drumming his claws and mumbling insults under his breath.

'It's ridiculous,' said Pongwiffy, through a mouthful of fungus sponge (Sharkadder's speciality). 'Nobody goes anywhere any more. I just walked here and the woods are practically empty. They're all in bed asleep because they were up all night watching stupid spellovision. Lovely cake.'

'Mmm,' said Sharkadder vaguely, adding, 'although I don't know why you've got such a thing about it. What's wrong with spellovision?'

'Everything! It's full of rubbish and it stops people doing things. It's taking over the world. Even the *Daily Miracle*'s full of it. I mean, look.' She pointed at the paper, which was spread on the kitchen table. 'A huge story about that smarmy newsreader, splashed all over the front page.'

'Sheridan Haggard,' said Sharkadder, rather dreamily.

'Yes, him. The colour of his stupid limousine, the name of his dog, where he goes for his holidays, where he buys his daft ties. As if anyone cared.'

'What *is* the name of his dog?' enquired Sharkadder casually.

'Ribs. Why? What does it matter?'

'I don't know. It's interesting.'

'No it isn't. Nothing about Sheridan Haggard is remotely interesting. He's just some Skeleton.'

'But you must admit he does have a lovely voice. Like velvet ...'

'Velvet, my bum!'

Sharkadder looked shocked, as well she might.

'And look at this!' shouted Pongwiffy, really worked up now. 'Here's a photo of that weather girl, wotsername, Brenda. She used to be the receptionist up at the Wizards' Club. I didn't think it'd be possible to sink any further.'

'Mmm. I like those little clouds she sticks on, mind ...'

'And look! They've even done away with the crossword! The whole back page is about tonight's programmes. *6 pm. Embalming with the Mummies. 7 pm. The News, with Sheridan Haggard. 8 pm. Zombie Decorating.* Good grief!'

'Actually, *Zombie Decorating*'s quite good,' said Sharkadder.

'What d'you mean, good?'

'Well, these Zombies paint a room. Then they sit and watch it dry. It's very – soothing, isn't it, Dudders?'

'How do you know all this?'

'Dudley and I watched it over at the twins' last night. They've got an extra-wide screen.'

'Really?' said Pongwiffy sharply. 'You didn't tell me.'

'Oh, I just popped in for a moment. I didn't stay long. I wanted to catch the news. Then I watched *Zombie Decorating* for an hour. Then there was *Gnome and Away*. Well, I couldn't miss that, could I?'

'What's *Gnome and Away*?'

'It's a soap opera. It's on every night.'

'A *soap* opera?' Pongwiffy, a born soap avoider, was appalled. 'What, they sing in the *bath*? What do they wear? Flannels?'

'No, no! It's nothing to do with soap. It's about these Gnomes, you see, who –'

'Enough with the Gnomes!' Pongwiffy hurled the paper into a corner. 'I don't want to know about Gnomes. It amazes me why anyone does. I'm a Witch. I'm interested in Witchy things. I thought you were too.'

'I am, I am!' protested Sharkadder. 'It's just that GNarleen's in love with GNorman, who's secretly going out with GNometta who's got a secret crush on GNeville and …' She caught Pongwiffy's eye. 'Well, anyway, it's good,' she ended, lamely.

'*Good!*' spat Pongwiffy. '*Good!* What I want to know is, what happened to old-fashioned entertainment? Playing charades, or singing songs round a piano? All this sitting in front of a box watching Gnomes, it's not healthy.'

'It's not just Gnomes. There's *Goblins in Cars*. I watched it at Macabre's. There's this tribe of crazy Mountain Goblins and they've got hold of these beat-up old cars and they race them.'

'I didn't know Goblins could drive.'

'They can't. That's the whole point. They bash into each other. It's hilarious. Macabre loves it.'

'I see,' sneered Pongwiffy. 'Car-driving Goblins bashing into each other hilariously. I see.'

'And, just for your information –' Sharkadder looked proud – 'Cousin Pierre's doing a cookery programme. Ten o'clock tonight, live from the Gingerbeard Kitchens. It's called *Pierre's Pantry*. Tonight, it's marzipan frogs.'

Despite herself, Pongwiffy was impressed. Pierre de Gingerbeard, the famous Dwarf chef, was Sharkadder's cousin, twenty-four times removed. He was an excellent cook. His marzipan frogs were amazing. She knew. She'd tasted them.

'All right,' she conceded. 'So maybe, just occasionally, there might be something worth watching. But mostly, it's rubbish. If I want to watch rubbish, I can look out of my window. You'd have to be mad to spend good money on a talking box.'

'Mmmm.'

'Why are you crouching by the door like that? Why don't you come and sit down?'

'It's all right. I like crouching.'

'What's in that crate you're trying to hide?'

'Hide a crate? Me?' twittered poor Sharkadder. 'Whatever can you mean?'

'Stand aside,' ordered Pongwiffy sternly. 'I want to see it.'

'No,' said Sharkadder.

'In that case, let me guess. Could it be a new cauldron, by any chance? Or a job lot of fish heads for Dudley? Hm? Or – this is just a wild stab, mind – *could it be a spellovision?*'

'Oh, all right!' cried Sharkadder, stamping her foot. 'So what if it is? I can have a spello if I want.'

'*Spello!*' mocked Pongwiffy. '*Spello!* What kind of a daft name is that? And you stood there agreeing with me and all the time you're standing in front of one.'

'I wasn't agreeing with you.'

'You weren't disagreeing either.'

'Oh, shut up.' Sharkadder's temper was up now. 'I was being polite, that's all. But quite frankly, I've had enough. You've finished the sponge so you can go. I've got some unpacking to do. And don't bother to come round later either. Dudley and I will be watching spello, won't we, Duddles?'

'Aye,' agreed Dudley. 'I likes the cat-food adverts.'

'All right, then,' said Pongwiffy, highly miffed. 'See if I care.'

'I don't care if you care or not.'

'And I don't care whether you care whether I care. So there.'

A little silence fell. The clock ticked. Dudley swore under his breath.

'So,' said Pongwiffy stiffly. 'Does this mean we're breaking friends?'

'I don't know. Probably. I'll think about it. Now go.'

'Shall I see you at the Coven meeting on Friday?'

'Haven't you heard? It's cancelled. There's a new show starting called *Fiends*. It looks terribly good from the clips, doesn't it, Duddles? It's all about this group of Fiends who sit and drink coffee and talk about each other's problems . . .'

Pongwiffy went home.

CHAPTER FOUR

A Fascinating Find

It had been raining, just as Brenda the weather girl had predicted. Mind you, it often rained in Witchway Wood, so the odds were in her favour. When Pongwiffy arrived back at the dump, the dampness had brought out the smells in force. A fox, made brave by her absence, stood nosing at an old cabbage that had escaped from a sack of rotten vegetables.

'Mmm,' murmured Pongwiffy. 'There's nothing to beat the smell of home ... *Oi! You! You leave that alone! What's here is mine!*'

The fox gave her a dirty look and slunk off, its eyes red in the moonlight.

'That's right!' jeered Pongwiffy. 'Clear off back to your daft den and don't come back!'

And just to make absolutely sure the fox got her point (and because she was in a bad mood anyway), she aimed a kick at the cabbage. It flew from the tip of her boot, sailed up and over the mountains of junk and landed with a . . .

. . . *plink*.

Now, cabbages can land with a thump or, occasionally, a splat, depending on how mouldy they are. But they never land with a plink. Unless the thing they land on plinks.

'Funny,' said Pongwiffy. Her eyes narrowed. Slowly, she raised her head and sniffed the air.

Now, as you know, smell is Pongwiffy's speciality. Smell fascinates her. She's good at it. Not only does she have her own unique odour, carefully honed over many years, but she actually has a very highly tuned nose. What came to it now was a new smell. It was faint, but it was there. The smell of varnish. And wood. With faint overtones of metal. There was something new in the dump – something she hadn't smelled before.

Using her nose as a guide, Pongwiffy left the path and began wending her way towards the source.

It didn't take her long to find. It lay half under the broken ping-pong table. It was covered with a thick layer of dust, but the shape was unmistakable.

'Oooh,' said Pongwiffy, picking it up. 'A guitar.'

It was. All but one of the strings were broken and two of the pegs were missing, and the neck wobbled, but it was still a guitar.

Pongwiffy stood, turning it over in her hands. Using her sleeve, she gave it a brisk little rub. The moon glinted on polished walnut. Experimentally, she plucked at the string.

Plink.

It really was a rather satisfying sound. She did it again.

Plink. Plink, plink. Plink, plink, plink, plink, plink, plink, plink …

'Vot in ze vorld you got now?' said a voice from behind. It was Hugo and he was clutching his *Little Book of Hamster Wit and Wisdom*.

'It's a guitar,' said Pongwiffy happily. 'I've just found it. Good, isn't it?'

'It only got vun string?'

'Yes. So? That's all you need to go plink. Listen.' *Plink.* 'See?'

Hugo looked less than impressed.

'Oh, come on!' cried Pongwiffy. 'It's great! Just look at it. It's an antique. Probably quite valuable.'

'Zen vy it in ze dump?'

'Well, obviously, it got thrown away by mistake. See here, look. It's got lovely patterns carved on the neck. A sort of raspberryish design. Who knows what famous person might have played this? It may even have belonged to Wild Raspberry Johnson himself.'

'Who?'

'Surely you've heard of him? Wild Raspberry Johnson, the famous Wandering Woodsman? Or Rasp, as we fans affectionately refer to him. He sort of rasps when he sings. He's got a gravelly sort of voice. Shame he's not around any more.'

'He gone? Vhere he go?'

'Dunno. He's a Wandering Woodsman. Probably wandered off. He was good, though, in his day.'

'Ven zis singing Raspberry play guitar, 'e can do more zan plink?'

'Of course!' scoffed Pongwiffy. 'But then, so will I. I just need to get it fixed, that's all. I'll take it along to the Witchway Rhythm Boys – they'll do it. It'll cost me an arm and a leg, mind. But it'll be worth it. Then I have to learn to play. But that'll be easy, because I'm very musical.'

'You are?' Hugo sounded surprised.

'Oh yes,' boasted Pongwiffy. 'It's in the blood. What's with all the questions, anyway? Every time you speak, you ask a question. Why?'

'*A vise 'Amster alvays ask questions. Many a truth falls from ze most unlikely lips.*'

'Is that a quote from your stupid book?'

'Suppose it is?'

'Are you implying that my lips are unlikely?'

'Suppose I am?'

'Are you going to speak in questions for evermore?'

'Suppose I do?'

'I'm going in,' announced Pongwiffy, bored now. 'I can't be bothered to play silly games with you. I'm going to have a good look at my guitar.' She smiled down at her new treasure and gave it another little rub. 'You know, it's funny I should find this now. I was just saying to Sharky that all the good old ways of amusing ourselves have gone. Hey! We could build a porch on the hovel. Then I can sit out in my rocking chair on hot evenings, looking out over the dump, with a glass of iced bogwater, playing my guitar. When I've learned, of course. But that shouldn't bother me, because I'm a natural . . .'

Chattering away, cradling the guitar in her arms, she marched back to the path, with Hugo trotting in her wake. He kept a firm grip on *The Little Book of Hamster Wit and Wisdom*. He had a feeling he was going to need it.

CHAPTER FIVE
Goblins in Cars

It was a Tuesday night, and the Gaggle of Goblins who lived in a cave on the foothills of the Lower Misty Mountains should have been out hunting. (Traditionally, they always hunt on a Tuesday. Traditionally, they never catch anything. They are probably the worst hunters in the entire world, but that doesn't stop them trying.)

However, on this particular Tuesday, most of them were laid up with a very nasty dose of the Squidgets. This is a malady common to Goblins, brought on by eating fermented nettle soup. Goblin digestive systems can handle nettle soup with no ill effects as long as it's fresh. But when it starts to ferment, that's when the problems start. Symptoms include embarrassing noises, headaches, runny noses and itchy ears. The only cure is to lie down and groan until it goes away.

Five of the seven Goblins were afflicted: Stinkwart, Slopbucket, Hog, Eyesore and Lardo. Only Plugugly and young Sproggit were unaffected. This is because they were fighting each other at the time and didn't notice the others finishing up the soup until it was too late. Just as well. A black eye is nothing compared to the Squidgets.

So. Plugugly and Sproggit had gone off hunting as usual, leaving their stricken comrades moaning in the cave. They said they'd be gone all night, so everyone was quite surprised when they came rushing back after only an hour or so, bursting with exciting news.

'Whassup?' croaked Eyesore, squinting at the dazzling moonlight that streamed into the cave. 'Ooh, me head. Shut the boulder, I can't stand the glare.'

'Yeah,' agreed Slopbucket, clutching his bucket. 'We's sick, remember? You is s'posed to come in on tippy toes wiv a bunch o' grapes, not all this runnin' an' shoutin'. What's all the fuss about anyway?'

Groaning, the sickly Gaggle struggled to a sitting position.

'We just seen sumfin' *good*,' burst out Plugugly.

'Was it a doctor?' asked Hog, scratching his ears like mad. 'A doctor in a white coat, wiv a stifflescope an' a big bottle o' anti-Squidget pills? That'd be good.'

'Nope,' said Plugugly. 'Better. Seen it wiv our own eyes, didn't we, Sproggit?'

'Yeah,' agreed Sproggit, nodding eagerly. 'Wiv our own eyes. Bofe of 'em. Go on, Plug. Tell.'

'Well,' said Plugugly, drawing it out for dramatic effect. 'W-e-e-ll, me 'n' Sproggit was checkin' de traps down in de woods . . .'

'. . . an' it was all quiet,' chipped in Sproggit.

'Yeah. It was. Nobody about. *Funny*, I says to Sproggit.'

''E did,' Sproggit assured the company. 'That's just what 'e said.'

'*Funny*, I says. An' we happens to be passin' dat ole Witch Macabre's cottage at de time, an' I says to Sproggit, '*Ere! What's dat funny blue light comin' out de winder?*'

'That's what 'e said,' corroborated Sproggit, nodding vigorously. '*'Ere!* 'e says. *What's dat funny light*, 'e says, *comin' out the winder?*'

'Yeah,' continued Plugugly. 'So we tiptoes up to de winder, right, Sproggit?'

'Right. We tiptoes up. An' we looks in, an' we sees it.'

'Sees *what*?' came the united chorus. For the moment, the Goblins had forgotten their illness and were sitting up, all ears. They had been confined to a cave for the last week or so, remember. This was heady stuff.

'It were a Big Magic Box,' explained Plugugly. 'And dere was movin' pictures on it. And guess what de pictures was? *Goblins in Cars!*'

There was an electrified silence.

'What – *real* cars?' breathed Stinkwart, unable to believe his ears.

'Yep.'

'What – Goblins in *cars*?'

'Yep.'

'You mean – *real* cars wiv *Goblins* in 'em?'

'Yep. Dey was drivin' dem,' Plugugly elaborated. 'Dey was racin' dem round an' round. Dey went, *vroooooom! Vrooooom! Eeeeeeeeeek!*'

Plugugly raced his hand to and fro in the air, simulating as near as possible the sight and sound of the racing cars. Sproggit, wild with excitement, joined in. They smacked palms in mid-air, miming a crash.

'*Piaaaoooooow!*' they cried. '*Boom! Ouch!*'

'Sometimes dey crash,' added Plugugly, by way of explanation.

'They do,' affirmed Sproggit. 'It's great.'

The rest of the Gaggle sat struggling with this for a bit. Goblins are not quick on the uptake. It was too much information in one go. Their brains were overloading.

'So, this Box you seed,' said Stinkwart, after a bit. 'It's Magic, you say?'

'Must be,' said Plugugly. 'Movin' pictures, what else? An' you know what? Dey all got 'em. De Witches, de Trolls, de Skellingtons – everyone. Everywhere you goes, dey all got a Magic Box so dey can watch *Goblins in Cars*.'

''Cept us,' added Sproggit, sounding bitter.

'Who were the Goblins in the cars?' Eyesore wanted to know. 'Do we know 'em?'

'Yep,' said Plugugly, crossly. 'We knows dem all right, an' we doesn't like dem. It's dat outlaw Gaggle up in de Misty Mountains. De ones wiv de levver jackets. De Grottys. Dey gatecrashed our cave warmin' dat time, remember? An' now dey is on de Magic Box. You shoulda seen dem showin' off. Just cos dey got cars.'

There was a lot of teeth-gnashing and resentful thumping of fists into palms at this. (Goblins are very competitive. The Annual Inter-Gaggle Punch-Up is a highlight in the Goblin calendar. The Grottys win every time. It is a sore point.)

'Them Grottys!' growled Hog. 'Wiv their cars an' – an' their jackets! Grrr!'

'Think they're tough!' sneered Lardo.

'They *are* tough,' Slopbucket reminded him. 'They won the Punch-Up Cup three years runnin'.'

'Sixty-five years runnin', weren't it?' disputed Eyesore.

'Three, six, seventy-nine, who cares?' said Slopbucket carelessly. 'We can't count anyway.' Which was true.

'Since when 'ave they 'ad cars?' asked Hog, sick with jealousy. 'Last time I heard, they only 'ad one little old rusty tricycle between 'em. 'Ow come they got cars now?'

''S not fair! 'S not fair!' shouted Lardo, and the others joined in as soon as they got the hang of the words.

'Know wot?' said Plugugly, suddenly. 'I fink I feel an idea comin' on.'

The chanting trailed off into a respectful silence. All eyes were on Plugugly. Goblins rarely got ideas.

'I bet I know what it is!' Sproggit said suddenly, nearly exploding with excitement. 'I bet you're gonna say *we* oughter get one o' them Magic Boxes an' bring it back up 'ere to the cave an', an', an' *watch* it every night, like everyone else. Am I right?'

'No,' said Plugugly, to everyone's surprise. 'Dat's

not it. What do we want an ole Magic Box for? We dunno where to get one an', anyway, we ain't go' no money so we'd 'ave to steal it. An' den dey'd find out we done it and take it away again. An' even if we did manage to keep it, knowin' our luck, somefin' 'd go wrong. We'd drop it or break it or de Magic'd turn on us or somefin'. We'd best steer clear o' Magic Boxes. Dey ain't a Goblin Fing.'

Actually, this was rather wise of Plugugly. Goblins and Magic are like bacon and chocolate sauce. They just don't go together.

'So what's the idea then?' asked Stinkwart. 'What *do* we want?'

'I'll tell you what we wants,' said Plugugly, slowly, importantly, aware that all eyes were on him. 'We Wants A Car.'

CHAPTER SIX

Obsession

Pongwiffy sat in her rocking chair, practising her guitar. The Witchway Rhythm Boys had done a good job (at a very steep price!). They had replaced the strings and fixed the neck. All the pegs were present and correct. It had been glued and waxed and buffed. Even Hugo had to admit it looked good.

Pongwiffy loved it with a passion. She carried it everywhere. She slept with it. She even *cleaned* it. Apart from eating, it was her favourite occupation.

She had moved on from plinking. Her new method of playing now consisted of sweeping her hand across the open strings, producing a horrible discord that clashed with itself, let alone whatever she happened to be singing.

Well, singing is a kind term. Pongwiffy's voice was a sort of tuneless honk that careered off on its own sweet way, regardless of melody, rhythm or anything at all, really.

The worst of it was, she thought she was good.

'*One witch went to woo,*'

honked Pongwiffy, strumming her discord.

'*Went to woo a wizard,*
One witch and her wand
Went to woo a —

AND WHERE HAVE THE PAIR OF YOU BEEN, MAY I ASK?'

Hugo and the Broom were standing in the doorway, attempting to sneak in without being noticed.

Pongwiffy carefully placed the guitar on the kitchen table, currently strewn with scribbled-on bits of paper (lyrics for her songs), stood up and looked stern. The Broom drooped and made abject little circles on the floor with its bristles. Hugo stood his ground.

'Well?'

'Novhere,' said Hugo, shortly.

Things hadn't been too good between the three of them recently. Hugo and the Broom were getting very tired of Pongwiffy's new hobby. Hour after hour, night after night, she sat crooning away, asking what they thought and forcing them to join in the chorus. Her obsession was becoming more than they could bear, which is why they had accepted an invitation from Vernon, Ratsnappy's rat Familiar, to go round and watch *Familiar Fortunes*, the new game show everyone was talking about.

'Yes you have. The two of you have been watching spellovision round at Ratsnappy's, haven't you? Don't tell me fibs because I know. I heard Vernon invite you when he thought I wasn't listening.'

'OK. Is true,' admitted Hugo, with a shrug. 'Ve go out to get avay from ze plinkink. Vot else ve supposed to do? I not even got nussink to read since you hide my book.'

'I didn't hide your book, *actually*,' said Pongwiffy.

This was true. She hadn't. She had thrown it away. Hurled it far into the rubbish dump when Hugo wasn't looking.

'Anyway,' she continued, 'anyway, I don't plink any more! I haven't plinked for days. That just shows how much interest you take. I've been experimenting with my technique and I sort of hit the strings now. I call it thrumming. Like this.'

She snatched up the guitar and demonstrated.

Thrummm!

'Plink, thrummm, votever, is horrible,' said Hugo. 'You not *fun* any more. Togezzer, ve used to make good Magic. Now you make bad music. I bored, I go out.'

'Well, you shouldn't!' scolded Pongwiffy. 'You're my Familiar. Your job is to help me in *all* my undertakings. *All.* That means listen to me practise. Tell me how good I am. Give me support and encouragement in my new career. You!' She turned to the Broom, which was dithering uncertainly in the background. 'Get in the cupboard. You're grounded.'

'Vot new career?' asked Hugo. A little wrinkle of anxiety crossed his furry brow.

'My new career as a singer–songwriter. I should have done it years ago. My old mum used to say I sang like a lark. Or was it a shark? Do sharks sing? Does it tell you that in your *Little Book of Wisdom*? Hm?'

'How I know? You hide it.'

'No I *didn't,* I tell you. Although you couldn't blame me if I had, because, let's face it, you've been neglecting your duties recently. Of course –'

she paused, considering – 'of course, I won't need a Familiar any more if I swap Magic for music.' She stared at Hugo for a long moment, then gave a snort of laughter. 'Oh, take that daft look off, I'm only kidding. I've missed you, actually. Put the kettle on and make us both a nice cup of bogwater. I'll sing you my latest song. It's about you – listen.

'My hamster lies over the ocean,
He left on a silly wee raft,
Forgetting to take any paddles,
Which just goes to show that he's –'

'Votch it,' warned Hugo. But he grinned a bit. He hopped on to the draining board and began busying himself with kettle and teacups.

'So. What's it like out in the woods tonight?' asked Pongwiffy.

'Quiet. Everysink cancelled due to lack of interest.'

'It's getting worse,' observed Pongwiffy grimly. 'Everybody's spellovision mad. Obsessed, that's what they are. Know what obsession is, Hugo? It's when people can't stop talking about one thing to the point where they become utterly boring. Now, shut up and listen to this. It's a song about my cauldron.

'*You are my cauldron, my rusty cauldron,*
You cook my dinner, it tastes OK.
The bits of rust-o I eat with gusto,
Please don't take my cauldron away ...'

Sharkadder was passing by, hurrying to get back to the evening spellovision feast. If Pongwiffy was obsessed with her guitar, Sharkadder was utterly addicted to spellovision. She simply couldn't drag herself away from it. The only reason she was out now was because her cupboards were bare. She had finally run out of absolutely *everything* and was forced to go shopping for the first time in ages. She was doing it on her own too. Dudley was laid up with a bad back and her Broom claimed bristle rash, although really they were both perfectly well and just wanted to stay home and watch *Familiar Fortunes.*

So. There was poor Sharkadder, struggling under the weight of four enormous shopping bags, three of which consisted entirely of tins of cat food. The handles were cutting into her fingers. She was wearing brand new spike-heeled boots with pointy toes and her feet were killing her. Every few steps, she had to stop and put everything down. To make it all a thousand times worse, each dwelling she passed had spellovision on.

Several times she had been tempted to knock and

ask if she could come in and watch, but, desperate though she was for spello, she was even more desperate for a cup of tea and knew that nobody would offer her one. Hospitality was at an all-time low since the advent of spellovision. Nobody could be bothered to leave the sofa.

It was during one of her rests that she heard the sound of distant honking coming through the trees.

'Oh, the grand old Witch of Rhodes,
She had ten thousand toads,
I said, please will you give me some?
I notice you have loads.
That Witch, she said to me,
"Those toads do not come free,
Go catch your own, you lazy crone!"
Fa lala lala lee ... Come on, you two, join in the chorus!
Oh, fa lala lala leee ...'

It was horrible, horrible singing, but it was music to Sharkadder's ears.

'Ah,' said Sharkadder. 'Of course! Pong'll be pleased to see me.'

And she limped off in the direction of Number One, Dump Edge.

*

Hugo opened the door.

'*Fa lala lala leeee* ...' Pongwiffy was warbling cheerfully in the background.

'Oh,' said Hugo. 'It you. You got zat bad old cat viz you?'

'No,' said Sharkadder humbly. 'Dudley's home watching spellovision. I was just passing, and I was wondering if Pong was busy.'

'Jah. She sink.'

The background honking broke off.

'Who is it, Hugo?' called Pongwiffy.

'Vitch Sharkadder. Viz lot of shoppink.'

'Really? Sharky? Oh, *good*!'

Pongwiffy appeared in the doorway, guitar in hand and best welcoming smile on her face.

'Hello, Pong,' said Sharkadder, slightly guiltily. It was the first time she had seen Pongwiffy since their row. 'Can I come in for a minute and rest my feet? It's these new boots. My toes feel like they've been sharpened.'

'Come in?' cried Pongwiffy, heartily. 'Of course you can come in. Old pal, old mate, old buddy.'

'Really? I thought you weren't speaking, after the words we had about You Know What.'

'Oh, pooh! Long forgotten. Hugo, get out another cup – we've got a visitor.' Pongwiffy peered down hopefully at Sharkadder's bags. 'Is there cake in any of those bags? By any chance?'

45

'Yes, actually. A chocolate one, which I'm saving for –'

'Good,' interrupted Pongwiffy approvingly. 'Plates, Hugo! Any biscuits?'

'Well, yes, some jammy ones I'm planning to have tomo–'

'We'll have them too. Hugo'll do it. Come on, I'll play you my guitar.' She led the way into the squalid hovel.

'I noticed the guitar,' observed Sharkadder, following behind with the bags. 'Is it new? You never mentioned you played.'

'Didn't I? Oh yes,' said Pongwiffy carelessly. 'I'm rather good, actually. Not quite in Wild Raspberry's class yet, but then, we have different styles.'

She began rummaging in Sharkadder's shopping, sorting out the things she liked.

'Er ... Wild Raspberry?' enquired Sharkadder, puzzled.

'Yes. I take it you're not a fan.'

'I prefer gooseberries myself,' said Sharkadder, confused. 'Especially in a flan.'

'Ah!' Pongwiffy emerged with a cake box and waved it triumphantly. 'Here we are, Hugo, get slicing. Sit down, Sharky, and I'll play you the song I wrote about you.'

'About me?' said Sharkadder, surprised and

flattered. She sank gratefully into the nearest chair. 'Really? You've written a song about *me*?'

'Oh yes. It's one of my better efforts. I call it "Nose Song".'

Pongwiffy threw herself into her rocking chair, played her horrible discord – *thrummmmmm!* – took a deep breath and burst into song.

> '*Of all the witches in the wood,*
> *There's none like good old Sharky.*
> *She wears a lot of lipstick*
> *In unusual shades of khaki.*
> *I love her very dearly*
> *And I'm glad I have a friend*
> *With a nose so long and pointy*
> *That you cannot see the end.*
> *Poi–nty!*
> *Poi–nty!*
> *Her nose is long and pointy*
> *And you cannot see the end.*'

Thrummmmmm!

'Why, thank you, Pong,' said Sharkadder. 'Nobody's written a song about me before. I'm really touched.' She scrabbled in her handbag for a hanky and dabbed at her eyes.

'You see?' said Pongwiffy. 'I look around me and

47

observe interesting things like people's noses, then compose songs about 'em. I wouldn't have written that if I'd been watching spello, would I?'

'You're right,' agreed Sharkadder humbly. 'You wouldn't. I'm terribly grateful, Pong.'

'So you liked it.'

'I loved it. Lovely words. Very — rhymey.'

'Lyrics. They're called lyrics, because they're set to music.'

'Oh, right. How does the tune go? Will you sing it to me again?'

Pongwiffy obliged. Then they had tea and cake while Hugo wrote the lyrics out neatly because Sharkadder wanted a copy to take home. Then Pongwiffy sang it a few more times, and Sharkadder joined in, in a shrill, wobbly soprano. Then they demanded more tea and cake, followed by biscuits. Then they talked about writing a second verse and called for more paper and ink.

That was when Hugo went to bed.

Much, much later, Dudley and the Broom were surprised when the door burst open and Sharkadder came flying in, scrabbled around in a drawer and emerged with an ancient harmonica before rushing out again, slamming the door behind her.

Well, they were surprised for half a minute. But

it took no time at all before they settled back to watching spellovision.

CHAPTER SEVEN
Gossip

Malpractiss Magic Inc. is a wandering shop that comes and goes as it pleases. This can be a bit inconvenient sometimes. However, you can usually catch it between the hours of midnight and dawn by the stream under the old oak tree. Some nights you might have to wait a bit while Dunfer Malpractiss, the owner, finishes serving the last customer in another dimension. But he and his shop generally turn up. He has a lot of regular customers in Witchway Wood.

This particular night – Friday – he was late, and a queue was forming by the patch of empty space where the shop currently wasn't.

At the front was a female Skeleton with a blonde

wig and a net shopping bag. She was avidly reading the latest article in the *Daily Miracle* about Sheridan Haggard (his favourite brand of soap and where he bought his bow ties).

Behind the Skeleton stood two large Trolls. They were discussing the latest programme to appear on their screens – a DIY show with a Troll slant entitled *Changing Bridges*. Both agreed it was much better than *Zombie Decorating*, which was getting a bit samey.

Behind *them* was a group of Witches: Bendyshanks, Ratsnappy and Scrofula. Guess what they were talking about? Right.

'It's undemanding, that's what I like about *Gnome and Away*,' Witch Bendyshanks was saying. 'No plot to speak of. All the characters are the same. Restful viewing, that's what it is. Like floating in warm treacle.'

'You can have too much treacle, though, can't you?' mused Witch Ratsnappy. 'I like the adverts myself. Better plots.'

'That's true,' nodded Scrofula. 'Although Barry and I like *Fiends*. And *The News*, with Sheridan Haggard, of course.'

'Oh yes,' agreed Bendyshanks and Ratsnappy. 'That goes without saying.'

'Such a lovely voice, hasn't he?' sighed Bendyshanks. 'I could listen to him all night.'

All three Witches had run out of things that you can munch in the dark on a sofa, and had come out to stock up. Unlike Sharkadder, who spoiled Dudley dreadfully, they had brought their Familiars along to help carry the bags – Bendyshanks's snake (Slithering Steve), Ratsnappy's rat (Vernon) and Scrofula's bald vulture, Barry. They too were talking about spellovision.

'Did you see *Familiar Fortunes* last night?' Vernon was asking.

'Too right I did,' said Slithering Steve. 'What's with that Toad family? Talk about thick.'

'Where do they find 'em, eh?' agreed Barry, adding wistfully, 'I wonder how you get to go on?'

'That'd be something, wouldn't it?' sighed Steve. 'To be on the spellovision.'

'That'd be something, all right,' nodded Vernon. 'We'd be famous then, eh?'

They laughed.

Just at that moment, the air gave a wobble and the Magic Shop appeared. It was rather like a caravan with a big cutaway section at the front where Dunfer served his customers. The blind shot up and there was the man himself, sucking on his moustache and leering unpleasantly over the till. The blonde Skeleton folded her paper, took out a shopping list and began pointing to various items on the shelves. The queue shuffled forward a fraction.

'I wish she'd hurry up,' said Bendyshanks. 'I want to get home. That weather girl, Brenda, said it might rain. Mind you, she always says that.'

'At least we're not missing anything good,' remarked Ratsnappy. '*Goblins in Cars,* that's all.'

'We don't like *Goblins in Cars,*' chorused two more voices. Agglebag and Bagaggle, the twin Witches, had joined the end of the queue.

'Me neither,' agreed Bendyshanks, Ratsnappy and Scrofula. 'Loada rubbish.'

(Witches and Goblins don't get on. *Goblins in Cars* was the one programme the Witches didn't bother watching, apart from Macabre, who had a violent streak, and Sharkadder, who would watch anything.)

'Here,' said Ratsnappy. 'Has anyone seen Pong-wiffy lately?'

'*I* heard she's come over all musical. Learning the guitar, I heard,' said Scrofula.

'Really?' said Bagaggle with a little frown. 'Did you hear that, Ag?'

'I did, Bag,' said Agglebag. 'I bet she's not as good as us.'

'Fat chance, Ag,' said Bagaggle. The twins played violins and mistakenly considered themselves very good at it.

'Sharkadder's been going round there most evenings, I hear,' contributed Scrofula.

'I thought they weren't speaking,' said Ratsnappy.

'Oh, they're all friends again now, apparently. Sharkadder's taken up the mouth organ. They're writing songs together.'

'Fancy,' said Ratsnappy. 'Seems a funny thing to do when you could be watching spello. Although I must say it's ages since I practised my recorder . . .'

In Number One, Dump Edge, Pongwiffy and Sharkadder were practising their new song. It was called 'What Shall We Do with a Rude Familiar?' and was intended to have a rollicking, seafaring sort of feel.

'Poke 'em in the dark with a sharpened chair leg Early in the morning!' they carolled merrily.

Pongwiffy played her discord again, several times. Sharkadder sucked and blew her mouth organ, producing a series of wheezy chords. Then they both sat back and smiled at each other happily.

'That's three songs we've co-written,' said Sharkadder. 'Three whole songs and we've only been at it for three days and nights. We're getting good, aren't we?'

'Good?' cried Pongwiffy. 'We're better than *good*. We're staggeringly, amazingly brilliant. Of course, I was writing good stuff *before* you started coming round, but I must say we make a good team. It's fun, doing things together again, isn't it?'

'It is,' agreed Sharkadder. 'I'd forgotten.'

'Better than watching spellovision. Go on, admit it.'

'I do,' said Sharkadder. 'You're absolutely right, Pong. There's nothing like old-fashioned, home-grown entertainment. Can we sing "Nose Song" again? It's still my favourite. And can I do another mouth organ solo between verses?'

'By all means,' said Pongwiffy graciously. 'After three. One, two, three.

'*Of all the Witches in the wood —*'

But just at that point, there came a knock on the door. This time, there was no Hugo to answer it. Rather tiresomely, he had gone missing again, for the third night running. So had the Broom.

'Oh, bother!' cried Pongwiffy, jumping to her feet. 'Who can that be? Hold that note, Sharky, I'll be right back.'

It was Ratsnappy, standing on the doorstep, holding a recorder in one hand and a large paper bag in the other.

'Hello, Pongwiffy,' she said. 'Can I come in? I just happened to be passing by with my recorder and this bag of delicious doughnuts.'

'I see,' said Pongwiffy, folding her arms. 'Nothing on spellovision?'

'Well – to be honest, I've been getting a bit bored with spello lately. I fancy a change. I heard you and Sharkadder were having musical evenings and I was hoping you might let me join in.' She held up the bag. 'They're *jammy* doughnuts.'

'Ah.' Pongwiffy loved jammy doughnuts. 'Funnily enough, I was thinking that the one instrument lacking was a recorder. In you come, Ratsnappy. Make yourself at home. Sharky! We're a trio!'

They had hardly got settled when there came another knock on the door. This time it was the twins, armed with their violins and two more paper bags. It was common knowledge that the way to Pongwiffy's heart was through her tummy.

'Bag and I have come for the musical evening,' announced Agglebag.

'We've brought our violins,' added Bagaggle.

'Hmm,' said Pongwiffy. 'What's in the bags?'

'Toffees,' chorused the twins.

'In you come,' said Pongwiffy.

And that was only the beginning ...

CHAPTER EIGHT
Plans

Witch Macabre and her Familiar, a Haggis called Rory, sat slumped on the tartan sofa, eyes glued to the screen. *Goblins in Cars* was on. A number of old, beat-up vehicles with numbers on were screeching around a racetrack, backfiring and shedding various bits – wing mirrors, doors, exhaust pipes, wheels and so on – as they took the corners at ludicrously high speeds.

Each car was driven by a demented Grotty who didn't care about anything except going *fast*. Forget danger, rules, pain, all that stuff. Speed was the thing. The race didn't appear to have a start, a finish, or any rules whatsoever. Engines regularly burst into flames. Every so often one of the drivers would take it into his head to screech to a halt, turn round and go the other way.

There were a *lot* of crashes. Not enough for Macabre, though.

'Aye!' bawled Macabre. 'That's it! Put yer cissy foot doon, Number Five! Aim for Number Three! Go on, go on! Faster, faster, bit left, straighten up, ye fool – och, blast! Missed. See that, Rory?'

'Aye,' scoffed Rory. 'Flippin' amateurs. Pass us a shortbread. Or have ye eaten them all?'

'Aye,' confessed Macabre. 'Ah think ah might have at that.'

'Your turn to go to the cupboard,' said Rory.

'Ach, nooo!' wailed Macabre. 'That means ah'll havtay *mooooove*!'

The sofa was away from the window, so neither of them noticed that they were not alone. Outside in the chilly night, who should be crouching in Macabre's toadstool patch, noses propped on the windowsill, jaws dropped, eyes on stalks, goggling in at the amazing Magic Box, but – the Goblins! They were over the Squidgets and had come to see for themselves whether or not Plugugly and Sproggit had been exaggerating about *Goblins in Cars*.

'See what I mean?' whispered Plugugly. 'Ain't it just – just de *best* fing you ever seed?'

'Yeah,' breathed Hog, Lardo, Eyesore, Stinkwart

and Slopbucket. Their boggling eyes were riveted on the flickering screen.

'Told ya, didn't we?' squeaked Sproggit. 'It's just like what we said, ain't it? About the Magic Box an' everyfin' – oof!'

He broke off as Slopbucket smacked a hand over his mouth.

From inside the room, there came a sudden noise like a miniature hail storm. Macabre had stood up and was emptying her lap of the evening's biscuit crumbs. As she did so, there came a strange, muffled cry from outside and a sort of urgent, disturbed, flapping noise, but when she moved to the window to investigate, there was nothing to be seen. She put it down to a night bird, drew the curtains and hurried to the kitchen on a quest for more shortbread.

Some time later, the Goblins arrived back at their cave. Plugugly heaved the boulder shut behind them. Then, quietly, with none of their usual fuss or argy-bargy, they all sat down in a circle.

They hadn't uttered a single word all the way home. Not one. Not even 'ouch' when they walked into trees. It was as though they were in a trance. They didn't argue or push or anything. Each was lost in his own thoughts. Well, thought. There was only room for the one thought, because it was such a big, overwhelming one. The thought was this:

CAR. WANT ONE.

Plugugly broke the silence.

'So now you know,' he said.

The Goblins nodded.

'Goblins in cars, just like we said,' added Sproggit.

More nods, and some drooling.

'C-a-a-r,' whispered Eyesore, drawing the word out slowly as though testing the feel of it in his mouth.

'Vroom, vroom,' agreed Slopbucket, faintly.

'Eepy, beep,' added Lardo dreamily, hands stretched before him, turning an imaginary steering wheel.

'Eeeaaaaaaaaw – *bang!*' contributed Hog, eyes closed as he relived one of the more spectacular crashes.

'C-a-a-a-r,' drooled Eyesore again. 'Want c-a-a-a-r.'

'Yes,' said Plugugly. 'We know dat, Eyesore. De fing *is*, 'ow is we going to get one? Dat's what we got to fink about.'

'C-a-a-a-r. C-a-a-a-a-r. C-a-a-a-a-r,' droned Eyesore, rocking to and fro.

'He's got stuck in a groove. Someone sit on 'is 'ead,' said young Sproggit.

Lardo obliged, and Eyesore's unhelpful contributions to the discussion became blissfully muffled.

'Come on,' said Plugugly. 'Fink. 'Ow do people get cars?'

'Buy 'em from a car shop?' suggested Hog.

'No car shops round 'ere,' said Plugugly. 'Besides, we 'asn't got no money.'

'Let's nick one,' suggested Lardo. Loud snores came from beneath his posterior. Eyesore was asleep.

'Oh yeah,' said Plugugly. 'An' what 'appens when dey find it gone? Den what?'

Blank faces all round.

'Dey'll come lookin' for *clues,* won't dey?' continued Plugugly, on a roll now. '*Clues* what will show who dunnit. An' straight away, dey'll see a dirty great big one.'

'What?' everyone asked.

'Us drivin' round in it. No point in 'avin' a car you can't drive round in.'

'Oh yeah,' said everyone, seeing the light. 'Right.'

'Seems like every plan we come up with 'as got a fatal flaw,' sighed Slopbucket. 'Can't buy one, can't steal one. I dunno.'

'P'raps someone'll give us one for a present,' said Hog.

'Who?' came the chorus.

'Santa?'

'Nah. Won't fit in the stockin',' Stinkwart pointed out.

'All right, the Tooth Fairy, then.'

'She only leaves *pennies,* stupid,' jeered Slopbucket. 'Since when 'as the Tooth Fairy left a car under yer piller? Stupid, you are.'

'Say that again,' said Hog crossly, 'an' I'll punch you really 'ard an' knock all yer teeth out and you can put 'em all under the piller an' maybe we'll get enough to buy a car after all.'

'Oh yeah?'

'Yeah!'

'Quiet, or I'll knock yer 'eads togevver,' threatened Lardo.

'Oh yeah?' (Slopbucket and Hog)

'Yeah!' (Lardo)

'Dere's only one fing we can do,' said Plugugly slowly, away in his own world, not even listening. 'It'll be hard, mind. But if we all work as a team, we might jus' pull it off.'

'Yeah?' said everyone. 'What?'

'We'll make one,' said Plugugly.

CHAPTER NINE
They're Playing Music!

'Beg pardon, Snoop? They're doing *what*?' bellowed Grandwitch Sourmuddle. She was watching *Fiends* on spellovision. The volume was up full because she was a bit deaf.

'Playing music in Witchway Hall, mistress. And singing,' bawled Snoop.

Snoop was Sourmuddle's Demon Familiar. He was small and red, with horns. Right now, he was toasting currant buns over the fire, using the prongs on his pitchfork. Sourmuddle hadn't bothered to go out for her meals for some time. In fact, she didn't even go into the kitchen. These days, she was rooted in the parlour, where she could adjust the volume to ear-splittingly loud and eat buns. (Buns, she had discovered, were ideal spello food, being too big to lose down the side of the sofa and more filling than peanuts.)

'What?' howled Sourmuddle. 'Speak up! They're doing *what*?'

Snoop reached out and turned the volume down.

'Singing. If that's what you call it. More like a cat's concert, if you ask me.'

'What d'you mean, singing? Who said they could sing?'

'No one, I reckon,' said Snoop, with a shrug. 'Why? Do you need permission to sing?'

'Most certainly, if you do it in Witchway Hall,' said Sourmuddle, firmly. 'Everything that goes on in there needs my permission. If you want to *breathe* in there, you need my permission. Who was there?'

'I don't know. I didn't stop to count. I was just passing. On my way home with the buns.'

'Well, you should have checked,' scolded Sourmuddle, wagging her finger. 'Whoever was there is breaking the rules. All bookings are supposed to go through me. Fetch the Bookings Book. I need to look into this.'

It took a while for Snoop to come up with the Bookings Book. Both he and Sourmuddle had become rather lax with the housework lately. Somehow, there never seemed to be a long enough gap between programmes to deal with it. Newspapers, magazines and mail just got dumped on the kitchen table, along with dirty coffee cups and screwed-up bun bags.

'You need to clear this place up a bit,' grumbled Sourmuddle from the sofa. 'I've just noticed what a tip it is. Come on, where's that book?'

'I'm looking, I'm looking, all right?'

Finally, he found it in the bread bin, of all places. He handed it to Sourmuddle with bad grace, then threw himself on to the sofa and settled down to *Fiends*.

Sourmuddle brushed off the crumbs, flipped the book open and ran a finger down the page. 'Nope. Just as I thought. Nothing down for tonight. Turn the spellovision off, Snoop.'

'Huh?'

'Turn it off.'

'*Huh?*'

'The spello. Turn it off.'

'Turn it *off*?'

'That's right.'

'But we never turn it off.'

'Tonight, we do.'

'But *Familiar Fortunes* is on next.'

'You've seen it; it's a repeat. Turn it off, we're going out.'

'Out? Out where?' said Snoop, confused. Going

out was a thing of the past, unless you were on the bun run.

'Where d'you think? To Witchway Hall. If there's illegal singing going on, I want to know *A*, why it hasn't been registered in the Bookings Book in a proper manner and *B*, why I haven't been invited. Now, where's my hat?'

Pongwiffy's musical evenings had proved unexpectedly popular – so much so that it was no longer possible to fit everyone into Number One, Dump Edge, which was a very *small* hovel and not really geared up for visitors. Every night for the past week, more and more wannabe band members had turned up on the doorstep, keen as mustard, waving bags of confectionery and begging to be let in. Musical evenings at Pongwiffy's were becoming the new In Thing.

'I'm sorry, no Familiars allowed,' Pongwiffy would explain airily on the doorstep to the latest supplicant. 'I'm running out of space. Besides, we've got enough singers. I'm restricting it to people who can play an instrument.'

'But I *can*!' the eager Witch would cry. 'Look! I've brought my castanets/triangle/spoons/comb and paper/bagpipes/Panamanian hip flute! And a bag of sherbet lemons. Oh, please!'

In the end, Pongwiffy always relented. She was a Witch of Dirty Habits who didn't get many visitors. It was a novelty, having all these people coming round with food bribes, begging to be let in the hovel instead of weeping to be let out.

'Oh, all right then,' she would say, rolling her eyes to heaven. 'If you *must*.' But she could never resist adding with a sarcastic little smirk, 'Although I thought you'd rather be at home *watching spellovision*.'

To which the sheepish visitor would generally respond with, 'Oh no! I wouldn't, really I wouldn't. I'd much sooner be here. I saw Sharkadder/Sludgegooey/the twins yesterday and they said it's fun. Oh, *please* let me in. I've brought a trifle ...'

Finally, when the number of band members swelled to twelve, it became clear that Pongwiffy's place really was too small. Nobody seemed to be using Witchway Hall these days, so it made sense to gather there.

Right now, they were in the middle of rehearsing a new song. Eleven chairs were arranged in a semi-circle facing the twelfth, on which sat Pongwiffy, loudly strumming her all-purpose discord. Attempting to play along with varying degrees of success were: Agglebag and Bagaggle (violins); Ratsnappy (recorder); Bendyshanks (castanets);

Scrofula (cowbell); Sludgegooey (comb and paper); Sharkadder (harmonica); Bonidle (triangle); Gaga (spoons); Greymatter (tambourine) and last and most certainly not least, Macabre on bagpipes.

The rehearsal was a bit of a shambles. Nobody seemed to know quite where they were in the new piece. It had been written jointly by Pongwiffy and Sharkadder and was entitled 'Witchway Stomp'. It featured a long harmonica solo and Pongwiffy's discord, played quite fast.

Ratsnappy, who could only play if she had the music, had lost it and was crawling about on the floor, searching. Sharkadder had stopped playing owing to a serious lipstick build-up in the holes of her harmonica. Sludgegooey's comb-and-paper combination was giving her troubles (disintegrated paper, toothless comb). The twins appeared to be playing a different piece altogether, although none of that mattered because Macabre's bagpipes drowned everything else out anyway.

The rhythm section was totally out of control. Gaga was sitting directly behind Scrofula and kept clonking her on the head with a spoon. Scrofula was hitting back with her cowbell. Bendyshanks hadn't quite got the hang of her castanets, but she was a queen of rhythm compared to Greymatter on the tambourine.

'Hang on, hang on!' Pongwiffy shouted over the cacophony. 'Stop! This isn't working. Sharky, what's happened to your harmonica? I can't even hear you.'

'Sorry,' called Sharkadder, poking around with a hairgrip. 'Lipstick stopped play. I'm just digging it out.'

'Well, hurry up. How can we keep in time if people keep dropping out just when they feel like it? Gaga, keep your spoons to yourself. Greymatter, please don't sing. You've got a voice like a toad with indigestion. Macabre, not so loud – it's giving us all headaches. Right, everybody, let's start again. Is anybody listening to me? Right. From the top. One, two – *ooooooer!*'

That was because there came a bang, a green flash and a very disgruntled-looking Sourmuddle appeared in their midst, holding a smoking wand. Snoop materialized at her side, holding the Bookings Book. Green smoke drifted around the stage, causing a lot of coughing.

'And what's all this about?' demanded Sourmuddle. 'Of course, I know I'm only the *Grandwitch,* nobody *important,* but maybe *somebody* might inform me as to exactly what's going on?'

'We're having a musical evening, Grandwitch,' explained Greymatter. 'Pongwiffy started it.'

'I see,' said Sourmuddle frostily. 'And why, may I ask, is it not entered into the Bookings Book?'

'We didn't think it was necessary,' admitted Pongwiffy. 'I mean, nobody's using the Hall these days, are they? All that space going begging. We thought we'd use it, that's all.'

'*We* did, did *we*?' snarled Sourmuddle. 'Funny how *we* never got round to mentioning these musical evenings to *me*.'

There was a guilty silence. It was true. Nobody had thought to mention the nightly gatherings to Sourmuddle.

'We hadn't seen you, that's all,' Pongwiffy hastened to explain. 'You're always cooped up indoors watching spello. We weren't trying to keep you out on purpose.'

'I should think not,' said Sourmuddle. Adding, 'Especially as I'm such a talented pianist.'

'You are?'

'Oh yes. Of course, I haven't played for years, but it's like riding a Broom. You never forget.'

And to everyone's astonishment, Sourmuddle climbed down into the orchestra pit, where the old piano had its permanent home. She whisked off the dust sheet, sat on the stool, opened the lid, cracked her knuckles, paused for a moment with her fingers suspended over the keyboard and her eyes closed – then lowered her hands and played.

She had a slapdash, who-cares-about-the-odd-wrong-note sort of style – but that didn't matter, because the tunes she played were jolly, romping, tinkley-tonkley ones, the sort that people sing standing on tables whilst hilariously showing their knickers. For the next ten minutes, the admiring Witches crowded round and tapped their feet. When she finally played the last, triumphant chord and smashed the piano lid down, everyone burst into spontaneous applause.

'Wow!' gasped Pongwiffy. 'That was *good,* Sourmuddle. And I'm talking as one musician to another. You can really tinkle those ivories, can't she, girls?'

The assembled company couldn't have agreed more.

'And there was me thinking *I* was good,' said Pongwiffy.

'Were ye?' said Macabre, rather unkindly. 'Nobody else was. Ye're rubbish, actually. Hands up who thinks Sourmuddle should be bandleader from now on?'

Everyone's hand shot up, apart from Pongwiffy's. Even Sharkadder's.

'Well, thanks very much,' said Sourmuddle briskly. 'A very wise decision. I'm sure I'll live up to the confidence you have placed in me.'

'Hey, hang on!' complained Pongwiffy, hurt. 'Whose idea was it, having musical evenings, in the first place?'

'Too bad. I'm Grandwitch and what I say goes. Right. Everyone bring your chairs down here and regroup round the piano. I'm taking over.'

'Don't take it to heart, Pong,' whispered Sharkadder. 'I think you're wonderful.'

'So why vote for Sourmuddle, then?'

'Well, I don't want to get into her bad books, do I? And neither do you. Look at it this way. If you don't have to be leader and worry about what everyone else is doing, you can concentrate on playing your chord, can't you? And we can still write our songs together.'

Pongwiffy thought about this. Actually, if the truth be known, she was quite relieved that Sourmuddle was taking over. Under her own control, things had been a bit ... well, chaotic, really.

'All right,' she conceded. 'Sourmuddle can be leader, I suppose. But I'm still chief songwriter. And I just hope nobody forgets that this was my idea in the first place.'

'What are you talking about?' enquired Ratsnappy, as they moved their chairs round the piano.

'The fact that the musical evenings were my idea,' explained Pongwiffy.

'Were they? I'd forgotten.'

By the end of the evening, though, Pongwiffy

had to admit that things were improving under the musical leadership of Sourmuddle. Sourmuddle had a good, solid left hand that maintained a steady beat. People didn't get so mixed up. Also, they behaved better. Gaga stopped playing Scrofula's head with her spoons. Scrofula kept her cowbell to herself. When Sourmuddle said to play a solo, solos got played. When people were told to sing up during the chorus, they sang up. To everyone's relief, Sourmuddle took Greymatter's tambourine away and sent her into a corner with instructions to write poetry.

They ended the evening with a vigorous, almost recognizable rendition of that old favourite, *When the Stoats Go Marching In*.

'Hey!' shouted Pongwiffy, all cheerful again. 'We're getting good. You know what? They ought to put *us* on the spello! We're a bloomin' sight better than most of the tripe they have on.'

Instant silence. You could have heard a pin drop. Everyone was thinking — hard. Finally, Sourmuddle spoke.

'Pongwiffy,' she said, slowly. 'I don't often go along with your ideas, which, quite frankly, are usually bonkers. But this time, I think you just might have something . . .'

CHAPTER TEN

An Important Meeting

At Spellovision Centre, in a grand boardroom full of polished wood and potted plants, an important meeting was taking place. The head of the studio, a portly Genie by the name of Ali Pali, was addressing his team, which consisted of five: the Star, the Cameraman, the Soundman, the newly appointed Head of Glamour and the Everything Else Boy, who was currently in charge of the tea trolley.

Clearly, the studio head wasn't best pleased. He sat at the top end of a long table, arms folded, scowling beneath his turban. Beside him was a portable blackboard, showing a graph with a steeply descending line. Before him was a pad, a feathered pen and inkpot, and several sharpened pencils.

'. . . and so, as you can see, the ratings continue to slide,' he was saying, in tones of deepest gloom. 'Not good. Not good at all. In fact, worse than not good.'

'That'd be bad, then,' said the Head of Glamour, who was none other than Brenda the weather girl.

'Well, I hope you're not blaming *me*,' drawled the Star, Sheridan Haggard, in his rich, golden-brown voice. '*I'm* still popular enough, if my fan mail's anything to go by. Aren't I, Ribsy? Isn't daddy a star?' He patted the small bundle of bones on his lap. This was Ribs, Sheridan's adored pet dog, who ate from a silver bowl and wore a bejewelled collar.

Ribs wagged his skeletal tail and gave a little woof.

'I am not *blaming* anyone,' Ali Pali told him wearily. 'I am just stating a fact. People are switching off. In the beginning, we could palm them off with any old rubbish, even *Zombie Decorating*. Novelty value, you see. But now, alas, boredom is setting in. Which is why I've called this meeting. We must decide which programmes get the chop, and come up with some new, exciting ideas quick, before I start losing money.'

The Cameraman – a pale Vampire called Vincent Van Ghoul – stuck his hand up.

'Mr Pali?' he said.

'Yes, Vincent?'

'I think we should cut *Goblins in Cars*. Nobody watches it. It came bottom in the viewers' poll.'

'Yeah. Vince is right – it's rubbish,' agreed the Soundman, a small, bad-tempered Tree Demon wearing earphones.

'Apart from anything else, it's dangerous to film,' added Vincent. 'They're crazy, those Grottys. Drive straight at us, don't they, TD?'

'I thought *I* was mad,' growled the Tree Demon.

'We should stop giving them cars,' continued Vince. 'It's irresponsible. Mindless violence. What if little kiddies see it?'

'Very well,' said Ali Pali. He took a pencil and made a note on his pad. 'Cut *Goblins in Cars*. Any more suggestions?'

'Well, of course, personally, *I* feel it would make sense to extend *The News*,' said Sheridan Haggard, never backward in coming forward. 'After all, it's me they want. By the way, will this take much longer? I have a skull polish at three. The limo's outside with the engine running.'

'Yes, well, of course, it would be. And at my expense, no doubt,' snapped Ali Pali, slamming down his pencil, which broke. Everyone stared. It was rare for him to lose his composure. The situation was clearly critical.

'Nice cup of tea, Mr Pali?' suggested the Everything Else Boy.

The Everything Else Boy was a small, wiry, energetic Thing in a Moonmad T-shirt. He had started out in spellovision as the tea boy, but people took advantage of his enthusiasm and his career had taken off. He was now make-up artist, set designer, production assistant, casting director and a whole host of other things too numerous to mention. But he liked making tea most. You knew where you were with tea. Plus, you got to wear a frilly apron.

'Good idea,' agreed Ali Pali. 'Tea would be good.'

The Thing raced to the trolley and started crashing about with cups.

'Sixteen sugars for me,' said the Head of Glamour, who had a large, dirty foot on the table and was painting her toenails pink.

'No tea for me. I only ever drink champagne,' announced Sheridan Haggard airily. 'And Ribs will have a bowl of fizzy mineral water, with half a slice of lemon.'

'What about *Zombie Decorating*?' went on Ali Pali, ignoring him. 'Chop or no chop? Vince? TD? What do you think?'

'Chop,' chorused Vincent Van Ghoul and the Tree Demon.

'And personally, I think we're overdoing the

Gnomes,' added Vincent. 'There are Gnomes in nearly every programme.'

'But Gnomes are cheap,' Ali Pali, ever the businessman, reminded him. 'Desperate to get into showbiz, Gnomes. You know what they say. There's Gnome Business Like Show Business.'

'Yeah, but they can't act,' the Tree Demon pointed out.

'Does that matter, though? *Gnome and Away* is still very popular,' mused Ali.

'Not as popular as *The News*,' Sheridan Haggard slipped in smoothly. 'They're calling me The Skeleton with the Golden Voice. It was in yesterday's paper. I take it you all saw the article?'

There was something very annoying about Sheridan Haggard. Vincent Van Ghoul and the Tree Demon caught each other's eye.

'Of course,' said the Tree Demon sourly, 'of course, *you* was actually second choice. Boss here tried to get Scott Sinister to read the news, but he was too expensive. Right, boss?'

'Ahhhh,' said Ali Pali, glibly sidestepping the question as the Thing in the Moonmad T-shirt came rushing up with a tray full of steaming mugs. 'Tea. Excellent.'

'Did you?' enquired Sheridan Haggard in tones of rich indignation.

'Did I what?' asked Ali Pali, sipping his tea.

'Did you try to get Scott Sinister?'

'Now, why would I do that when I have you at half the price, Sheridan? Besides, he's away on location, as you well know, since you are currently renting his castle.'

This was true. Scott Sinister, the famous film star (and, incidentally, Pongwiffy's dream boat), was currently off making *Return of the Avenging Killer Poodles V.* Sheridan Haggard was renting Sinister Towers, Scott's holiday home, in order to be near the studio.

'I said no tea,' complained Sheridan Haggard, flinching as a chipped mug was dumped before him. 'Where's my champagne?'

'I can't afford champagne,' snapped Ali Pali sharply. 'Not after your last pay rise. You are costing me a fortune, Sheridan, with your exotic celebrity lifestyle, your fancy ties and your fancy car and your expensive drinks. I'm a hard-bitten business Genie. You'd better be worth it. You'd better hope your popularity lasts.'

'Ooh,' said Sheridan to the room in general. 'Get *him.*'

'I am just saying. And while we're on the subject, I'm not paying out for your entourage any more. Your butler and your chauffeur and your minders. You have to get rid of them.'

'But who will do all the work?' cried Sheridan, horrified. 'I am a *professional newsreader*! I must have *some* help. What will my fans think?'

'Hmm. Well, I'll think about it. All I am saying is, don't push your luck. Now then. Back to business. Ideas for new programmes. Head of Glamour? Any suggestions?'

'You what?' said Brenda, beginning on her second foot.

'You have just been made Head of Glamour, Brenda. You are meant to cover the female angle and come up with glamorous ideas.'

'What, now? While I'm doin' me feet?'

'Never mind, dear,' said Sheridan Haggard spitefully. 'You stick to what you're good at.'

'What about Luscious Lulu Lamarre, the actress?' suggested Vincent Van Ghoul. 'Couldn't we get her? She could do an hour's special. Singing and dancing and showing her talents. Right, TD?'

'Cor, yeah,' said the Tree Demon, brightening up.

Sheridan Haggard frowned. He didn't want famous actresses stealing his thunder.

'Sadly, we can't afford her,' sighed Ali Pali, and Sheridan relaxed. 'Besides, I ask myself, do we *need* a star? What do the viewers really *want*? Yes, thank you, Sheridan, I know they want you. But what else? Know what I think? I think they want programmes with the common touch. They want to see people just like them on spello.'

'So,' said Vincent reflectively. 'You're saying we need a programme that'll appeal to everybody.'

'Exactly. Something with the common touch. And preferably cheap. So don't suggest sending people off to faraway islands or quiz programmes where we give away money.'

'What about a sporting event?' suggested Vincent thoughtfully. 'A marathon, or something?'

'Hmm. Not everyone likes sport. But a competition of some sort – that's a good idea. Something like . . . like . . .'

Everyone blinked at the sudden flash of green light, followed by a thick cloud of evil-smelling smoke. Ali Pali choked on his tea, Brenda spilled her nail varnish and Ribs clattered down from his master's lap and hid under the table.

'Singing Witches,' finished off Pongwiffy, briskly stepping out of the green murk. She tucked her wand away and stared around at the startled company, who were busily choking and mopping up spills. 'That's what you need.'

'Oh,' said Ali Pali, wiping his streaming eyes. 'It's you, Pongwiffy. And that ridiculous Hamster.' He sounded glum.

'Hey,' said Hugo, from Pongwiffy's hat. 'Vatch it.'

(It should be explained that there is quite a bit of history between Pongwiffy and Ali Pali. Their paths have crossed before. They have a wary respect for each other's talents, but are not what you would call good friends. The same can be said about Vincent Van Ghoul, the Tree Demon, Brenda and the Thing in the Moonmad T-shirt, all of whom have had previous dealings with Pongwiffy.)

'You're darn right it's me. How's it going, Pali? I might have known you'd be behind this spellovision racket. It's your sort of thing, isn't it? Always got an eye open for the main chance. And look who's here! Vincent Van Ghoul and the Tree Demon, wouldn't you know. Well, well, well. Hey, you!' She pointed at the Thing in the Moonmad T-shirt. 'I'll have a mug of tea, if there's one going.'

'What are you doing here, Pongwiffy?' demanded Ali Pali wearily. 'This is a private meeting. You can't just come barging in.'

'I've come with a message from Grandwitch Sourmuddle. She says we Witches want to be on spello and you've got to come and make pictures of us singing or she'll want to know the reason why.'

'I'll tell her why,' said Ali Pali. 'Because nobody would watch it, that's why.'

'Witches would,' pointed out Pongwiffy reasonably.

'But not all viewers are Witches, are they? What about the rest of the viewing public? Can you see anyone else tuning in to hear Singing Witches? Vincent. You're a Vampire. Would you?'

'I'd sooner lie on a sunbed eating a garlic sandwich,' said Vincent Van Ghoul.

'But we're good!' argued Pongwiffy. 'Better than the other rubbish you show. Tell them, Hugo. Aren't we good?'

'It's not a question of good or bad,' explained Ali Pali. 'It's a question of what the viewers want. If you really want to know, I am *looking* for new programmes. If I thought Singing Witches would make people switch on, I'd be most happy to send the crew along. But, sadly ...'

'Shhh,' said Pongwiffy. 'Stop yapping. My Familiar wants a consultation.'

Hugo had dropped on to her shoulder and was tugging at her earlobe. Pongwiffy inclined her head, and he proceeded to hiss in her ear. As he talked, a grin began to spread across her face.

Sheridan Haggard, the only one who didn't know Pongwiffy, said, in his most pompous golden tones, 'My dear madam, I don't know who you are, but I really don't think ...'

'Didn't you hear?' said Pongwiffy, staring at him coldly. 'We're consulting.'

Sheridan subsided. The Thing shoved a mug of tea into Pongwiffy's hand. She took a loud slurp, then listened some more, nodding and grinning as Hugo whispered. Another minute or so dragged by. And then, 'Got it!' cried Pongwiffy triumphantly. She thumped on the table. Ali Pali's inkpot crashed to the floor. 'A Song Contest!'

'What?'

'A *Spellovision* Song Contest. It's brilliant. Everyone gets the chance to enter an original song.' Again, Hugo whispered in her ear. 'Well, everyone except Goblins, of course. And you film it while it happens and then the public votes for their favourite.'

Hugo whispered again.

'Better still,' continued Pongwiffy, 'there could be specially selected juries. And a really good prize for the winners, like a big silver cup and a week's all-expenses-paid holiday at Sludgehaven-on-Sea. You could get someone famous to present it.'

'Well, of course, I suppose I *could* –' began Sheridan Haggard, but he was cut off by Pongwiffy.

'I mean *really* famous. A *proper* star. Not some minor celebrity with a daft voice.'

'Now, look *here* . . .'

'Scott Sinister, for example. He's a friend of mine.'

This wasn't strictly true. By no stretch of the imagination was the famous star Pongwiffy's friend.

'Hah!' sneered Sheridan Haggard. 'A likely story!'

'But the money!' fretted Ali Pali. 'The studio's been losing money hand over fist. All those prizes . . .'

'Ah,' said Pongwiffy uncertainly. 'Yes. Well. I expect I'll think of an idea of how you can solve that. Won't I, Hugo?'

'Jah,' said Hugo, who was tired of whispering. He spoke to Ali directly. 'Easy. You make it pay for itself. Charge ze advertisers. Zey pay big money to get zeir product on zat night. And get live audience to come and votch. Charge zem too. Offer special deal on spello sets. Lots of publicity. Lots of pizzazz!'

'He's right, you know,' said Vincent Van Ghoul to the Tree Demon. 'It could work.'

'*She's* right, you mean,' Pongwiffy corrected him. 'This is *my* brilliant idea, you know. So what do you think?'

She directed the question at Ali Pali, who was currently sucking his flashiest medallion and staring into space. He gave a little start and came back to earth.

'What do I think? I'll tell you what I think.' He held out his hand. His mouth split, revealing a lot of white, shiny teeth. 'Pongwiffy, allow me to congratulate you. It *is* a brilliant idea. An *inspiring* idea. In fact, I wish I'd thought of it myself.'

'You do?' said Pongwiffy, preening a bit. (Flattery didn't come her way often.)

85

'I do. Perhaps we can put our differences behind us and you would consider becoming my head of programming – and your Hamster, of course?'

'I'll think about it,' promised Pongwiffy, 'but I don't hold out too much hope. I'm not sure I can fit it in. My music is all-consuming. I've given you the grand idea; it's up to you to work out the details. As long as we Witches win, I don't care. Now, you'll have to excuse me. I've got a song to write.'

CHAPTER ELEVEN
Sheridan Haggard, Newsreader

It was the following evening. Sheridan Haggard sat at the dining table in Sinister Towers reading the latest article about himself in the *Daily Miracle*. He was wearing a crimson silk kimono embroidered with skeletal dragons. Gold-framed reading glasses perched on the bony ridge between his eye sockets. Expensive rings flashed on his metacarpals (finger bones to you). Ribs sat on an expensive Persian rug, chewing a bone, of all things.

'Listen to this, Thing,' commanded Sheridan. 'There's another big piece about me in the paper.'

The Thing in the Moonmad T-shirt was currently clearing away the supper dishes. His job as Everything Else Boy had recently expanded to being

Sheridan's entire entourage. He was chief cook and bottle washer, chauffeur, valet, skull masseur, minder – well, you get the idea. By replacing Sheridan's posse of grovelling attendants with the Thing, Ali Pali had neatly solved the problem of how to save money and keep Sheridan happy at the same time.

Right now, the Thing was in butler mode. He wore a dark suit and a bow tie. At his master's command, he obediently set down his tray and adopted a polite listening pose.

'*Sheridan Haggard, the Golden Voice of spellovision, will be opening Wraithways, the new supermarket, shortly before midnight tonight,*' read Sheridan Haggard. '*Large crowds are expected. The popular newsreader has really caught the public's imagination, with his velvet tones and polished charm. It is to be hoped he will be bringing along Ribs, his charming little dog, a firm favourite with the kiddies.* Hear that, Ribs? Children love you.'

'Woof,' said Ribs, worrying his bone.

'Will I need me chauffeur's hat, boss?' asked the Thing. He had a lot of hats and small props. It was the only way he could remember who he was supposed to be.

'Most certainly,' agreed Sheridan. 'Clear away the dishes, set out my white shirt and opera cloak, then bring the limo round. Go on, hop to it. I can't be late. I'm an important man. After I've opened the supermarket, I have to be back in the studio in time for *The News*. I live for those bulletins, you know. It's only before a camera that I become truly alive.'

The Thing scooped everything on to the tray and hurtled out through the door.

Sheridan rose to his feet and stretched luxuriously. This was the life! Champagne and caviar on tap. A chauffeur-driven limousine. Flattering articles in the paper. Cheering crowds whenever he showed his skull in public. A huge salary and an enormous expense account which enabled him to rent a grand castle like Sinister Towers. And all because he happened to have a rich, golden–brown voice.

Lucky or what?

A short time later, dressed in frilly shirt and sweeping cloak, Sheridan stood before the castle gates, Ribs in his arms, waiting for the Thing to bring up the limo.

As always, a small crowd of die-hard fans was there to witness his departure. The Skeleton with the blonde wig was there, holding a bunch of wilting daisies. There was a Troll family, consisting of mum, dad, grandma and two small, shy Troll toddlers. Dad had a camera. The toddlers clutched autograph books.

'Go on, Gravella, ask him!' hissed the mother

Troll, giving the girl toddler a shove. You could tell she was a girl because she was wearing a pink sunbonnet. She took her thumb out of her mouth, toddled forward and thrust out the book. Ribs liked children. He wagged his tail and gave a happy little woof.

'Pleathe, thir, can I have your autograph?' whispered little Gravella shyly. The dad Troll readied his camera.

Sheridan looked down from his great height.

'Not now, small girl,' he said haughtily. 'I'm not in the mood.' And he stared pointedly up at the moon, tapping his foot impatiently.

Tears welled up in little Gravella's eyes. She flushed, looked around uncertainly, then walked back to her family and buried her face in the folds of her mother's frock.

There came a low purring, a glint of moonlight on polished chrome and the long black limousine slid up the gravel drive and through the gates. The Thing was at the wheel, wearing leather driving gloves and a chauffeur's hat perched at a jaunty angle. He jumped out, leaving the engine running, and scuttled round to open the back door. A rich smell of leather wafted from the interior.

Sheridan folded his tall frame and climbed in, placing Ribs on a special cushion. The door clicked shut and the Thing hopped back in the driver's seat. The Skeleton with the daisies moved forward hesitantly, holding out her flowers, then leapt back with a startled cry as the car moved purposefully forward. The bunch of daisies fell to the ground and was thoroughly mashed by the back wheel.

'So tedious,' sighed Sheridan, as the limousine picked up speed and the little group of fans receded into the distance. 'No respect for privacy. Have they never heard the phrase, *A Skeleton's home is his castle*?'

'Ain't strickly *your* castle, though, is it, boss?' observed the Thing, steering efficiently around the trees. 'Belongs to Scott Sinister.'

'Hah!' Sheridan let out a short, derisive bark. Ribs looked up anxiously, then went back to crunching the jewels off his collar. 'Don't mention that name to me.'

'What, Scott Sinister?'

'I said don't mention it!'

'Why not?' enquired the Thing innocently, honking at a rabbit.

'Because the man's an overrated charlatan, that's why.'

'Oh, I dunno,' argued the Thing, nudging the car on to the main trail, which wound through Witchway Wood. 'He was good as the daddy in *The Mummy's Curse*.'

'I didn't see it,' sniffed Sheridan.

'He was good. Course, he dropped off a bit after *Return of the Avenging Killer Poodles IV.* But they say the next one's gonna be a cracker. And that leadin' lady of his, that Lulu Lamarre, she's a bit of all right an' all.'

'Look,' said Sheridan through tight jaws, 'I said I didn't want to talk about him. The only good thing about Sinister is his castle, which I must admit is quite comfortable. But then, so it should be, with the exorbitant rent he's charging. Drive faster, we're late.'

'He's a proper star, though, ain't he?' persisted the Thing, who was indeed a fan. 'You gotta admit it. Why, he's got the whole world at his feet – *oi!*' Brakes were suddenly applied, the limo slowed to a crawl, and the Thing wound down the window and leaned heavily on the horn. 'Out of the way, losers!'

Seven figures were directly ahead, trudging along the middle of the road. They halted and stared over their shoulders, caught in the glare of the headlights like startled rabbits.

'Now what!' exploded Sheridan.

'Goblins,' said the Thing with a grin, hunkering down and revving the engine. ''Old tight, boss. I'll scatter 'em.'

He pressed the accelerator and the limousine

leapt forward, sleek, smooth and deadly as a car-shaped panther.

The Goblins scattered all right. With wild little squawks and howls, they dived for the bushes. Horn blaring, the limousine carved a path through them and vanished in a cloud of dust and exhaust smoke.

There was a short pause. Then, one by one, seven Goblin heads emerged from the bushes.

Now, you would expect them to be furious, wouldn't you? Mown down like that, without any warning. But they weren't. Oh no. Their faces wore the same trance-like expression as when they had been watching spellovision through Macabre's window.

As one, they faced the point in the distance where the limousine had vanished. Then, slowly, as one, they said, in tones of deepest admiration and envious wonderment, '*Phwoarh!*'

CHAPTER TWELVE
Song Writing

'We haven't seen each other for a bit, have we, Hugo?' observed Pongwiffy. She was sitting in her rocking chair, guitar cradled in her arms, waiting for Sharkadder to come round to visit. 'Not since music took over my life.'

'Mmm,' mumbled Hugo. He was sitting in the chipped sugar bowl, frowning down at a tiny pad of paper and pulling on his whiskers. A pencil stub was in his little pink paw.

'I mean, we *see* each other,' continued Pongwiffy, 'around and about. But we haven't had a proper chat for ages.'

'Mmm.' Hugo tapped his teeth with the pencil.

'So. How *are* things? What have you been up to?

I expect you're getting a bit bored with all this time on your paws. What with us not doing any spells and you having nothing to read now your daft little book's lost. I expect you'd probably like me to give you a task to do. Like put the kettle on.'

Hugo looked up, brow furrowed. 'Vot?'

'I said put the kettle on. Sharkadder'll be here any minute. I expect she'd like a cup of bogwater before we get started. We're working on our original song tonight. For the Song Contest. Nothing like bog-water to oil the brains.'

'You put it on. I busy.'

'No, you're not. You're sitting in a sugar bowl,' Pongwiffy pointed out. 'If that's busy, I smell like a rose garden.'

'I write,' said Hugo, waving his pad. 'See? I busy.'

'Oh,' said Pongwiffy. 'I *see*. It's *writing* now, is it? And what are you *writing*, may I ask? A letter to your stupid rodent relations? The world's first Hamster novel? What's it called? *The Boring Adventures of Fluffy*?'

'If you must know,' said Hugo, stiffly, 'I is composink a sonk.'

'I *beg* your pardon?' Pongwiffy frowned. 'A *song*? I thought *I* was the songwriter around here. Why are *you* writing a song?'

'Vy you sink? Cos ve is entering ze Sonk Contest, of course.'

'*We*, meaning?'

'Ze Familiars.'

'The *Familiars*?' Pongwiffy let out a rude cackle. 'Entering the Song Contest? Don't make me laugh!'

'And vy not?' snapped Hugo.

Pongwiffy stopped laughing. You had to be careful with Hugo. He had a short fuse.

'Everyvun else is. Ze Trolls, ze Gnomes, ze Banshees, ze Skeletons …'

'Gosh. Really?'

'Oh jah. It very popular. Zere goink to be strong competition, I sink.'

Pongwiffy didn't know whether to be pleased or worried. It's always nice to have ideas that are popular. On the other hand, strong competition meant that the Witches might not necessarily win.

Just then there came a knock at the door, followed by a shrill, '*Cooooeeee! Only meeeee!*' And in came Sharkadder, wearing a long purple cloak and matching purple ankle boots. She was carrying a purple lace parasol, a purple handbag, a special purple drawstring bag in which she kept her harmonica and a large cake box. Much to Hugo's disgust, Deadeye Dudley was with her, swishing his tail and glowering at everyone.

'Hello, Pong, sorry we're late,' said Sharkadder,

looking around for somewhere to sit. It was a choice between the sofa, which was currently sprouting a fine crop of mushrooms, or a three-legged chair on which had been dumped a half-finished plate of skunk stew, a collection of dirty socks and a wide-open tin displaying the warning: *Fishin Maggots. Kepe Furmly Clozed*.

'Have a seat,' said Pongwiffy.

'I'm trying to – I'm just picking off maggots. My, it's disgusting in here. I brought Dudley along because he wants to write a song with Hugo.'

'No, I don't,' growled Dudley.

'Yes you *do,* Duddles. Remember what Mummy said? You have a lot of musical talent. There's no reason why you and Hugo shouldn't work happily together, just like Pong and me.' She beamed at Pongwiffy and added, 'The Familiars are entering for the Contest, did you hear?'

'I heard,' said Pongwiffy.

'I told Dudley they should do one of his sea shanties.'

'Over my fluffy body,' sneered Hugo.

'Ah, shut yer gob, small fry!' spat Dudley.

'Say zat again, fleabag!' Hugo shot out of the sugar bowl and squared up.

'Small fry! Squirt! Daft little fur ball!' obliged Dudley.

'Mangy old vindbag! Mummy's boy! You sink you tough? I keel you!'

'Is that so? Listen, sonny, if 'twasn't for my bad back . . .'

'Listen to them teasing each other,' said Sharkadder fondly. 'It's a good thing they don't mean it.'

'I suppose we'd better get on,' said Pongwiffy. 'You've brought a cake, I see. Put the kettle on while I tune my guitar.'

With a little sigh, Sharkadder went to light the gas while Pongwiffy pretended to fiddle with the tuning pegs. In the background, Hugo was poking Dudley with the pencil stub, while Dudley tried to flatten him with his paw.

'I must say that things have improved now Sourmuddle's taken over,' remarked Sharkadder over her shoulder. 'At least she's keeping everyone in order. Things were getting a bit out of hand before, don't you think?'

'True,' admitted Pongwiffy. 'Thank badness she took those spoons away from Gaga.'

'Absolutely. And stopped Greymatter singing. Now Sourmuddle's in charge, you and I can concentrate on what we do best. Which is being creative and coming up with the winning song.'

This was true. Sourmuddle had lost no time in

getting everyone organized. Everybody now had a proper role in the band and it was working much better. The line-up went like this:

Sourmuddle — band leader and piano
Pongwiffy — guitar and writer of winning song
Sharkadder — harmonica and co-writer of winning song
Ratsnappy — recorder
Twins — violins
Macabre — bagpipes (but not so loud)
Bendyshanks — backing vocals/percussion
Sludgegooey — backing vocals/percussion
Scrofula — backing vocals/percussion
Bonidle — drums
Gaga — go-go dancing
Greymatter — mouthing the words

'Mind you,' said Pongwiffy, 'I'm still not sure about Bonidle on drums. Drummers aren't supposed to fall asleep between verses, are they?'

'She snores very rhythmically, though,' pointed out Sharkadder. She took two chipped mugs of bogwater to the cluttered table and found room between the piles of scribbled-on paper. She removed the stew, socks and maggot tin from the three-legged chair, drew it up to the table, spread out a clean purple hanky and sat down carefully.

'Aren't we having the cake?' asked Pongwiffy hopefully.

'Work first, cake later,' said Sharkadder, firmly. 'We have to take this seriously. You said so yourself.'

'Oh, absolutely,' agreed Pongwiffy hastily. She didn't want anyone thinking she didn't take song writing seriously. Although a bit of cake would have been nice.

In the background, the door slammed. Hugo and Dudley had taken their argument outside.

'Right,' said Sharkadder. She opened her bag and took out her harmonica, a clean pad and a nicely sharpened pencil. 'First things first. Are we absolutely sure we can't do "Nose Song"?'

'No. I keep telling you. It has to be a *new* original song.'

'All right,' sighed Sharkadder. 'OK. New song. Are we starting with the tune or the words?'

'The words,' said Pongwiffy, firmly. Tunes were all the same to her, but she had a fine appreciation of words, being a talkative type.

'I agree,' said Sharkadder. She wrote WORDS on her pad and underlined it. 'What should our song be about, do you think?'

Pongwiffy considered. Until now, most of her songs were rude ones about Hugo or boastful ones about the superiority of Witches. She had a feeling these were specialist interests. Witches would relate to them, of course, but the general public would want something a bit more – well, general.

'I'm not sure it has to be *about* anything,' she said. 'I think it just needs to be easy. Something you sing in ... places where people sing.'

'Like in the bath, you mean.'

'Don't say that word,' said Pongwiffy with a shudder. 'I mean, something undemanding. With lots of repetition.'

'You mean meaningless?'

'Well – yes. Meaningless, but catchy.'

'Right.' Sharkadder wrote it down. '*Meaningless – but – catchy*. Like what?'

'I dunno.' Pongwiffy cast about desperately. 'Like ... I dunno ... bing, bang, bong or something.'

'Bing, bang, bong,' nodded Sharkadder, scribbling away. 'OK. I've got that.'

'Or bong, bang, bing,' improvised Pongwiffy. 'Just as a variation.'

'Good idea. Or – this is just a suggestion, mind – what about bing, bong, bang?'

'Not bad,' agreed Pongwiffy. 'Not bad at all.'

'Or,' added Sharkadder, excitedly, '*or* even banga-langa binga-linga bonga-longa bing bong? Or is that going too far?'

'No, no,' said Pongwiffy. 'I think we can use it. Write it down.'

'*Or*,' suggested Sharkadder, really getting carried away now, '*or*, how about binga linga banga langa bonga longa rum dum, rama dama root toot, ding dong do?'

'Mmm. Getting a bit fancy now. But maybe it'll slip in somewhere. Stick it down, just in case.'

'We're getting on well, aren't we?' said Sharkadder happily. 'It's fun collaborating, isn't it, Pong? Don't you agree?'

'I would if I knew what it meant,' said Pongwiffy. 'Shall we have the cake now?'

CHAPTER THIRTEEN

The Competition

It wasn't only in Number One, Dump Edge, that preparations for the Song Contest were underway.

The Wizards' Clubhouse (think pointy turrets and lashings of gold paint) stands on top of a hill in the Northern Misty Mountains range. Despite erratic local weather conditions, the Wizards get an excellent spellovision reception. In pride of place in the lounge is a set with the biggest screen you have ever seen.

Wizards love spellovision. They have taken to it like flies to a jam sandwich. They spend most of their waking hours slumped in armchairs waiting for the next meal anyway, so watching spello is the ideal way of passing the time. Nobody does the crossword puzzle now. Nobody reads. Nobody makes wise, Wizardly comments in loud voices. Conversation is a thing of the past.

Well, it was until Sheridan Haggard announced the forthcoming Spellovision Song Contest on the news. That got them talking all right.

'... and specially selected juries will vote for the winner,' explained Sheridan in his golden-brown voice. 'Each faction is invited to submit a specially composed song. This can be performed by a soloist, or it can be a group effort. The contest is open to all, except Goblins. Entry forms are available from Spellovision Centre, at the address displayed below on your screens.

'The idea for a Spellovision Song Contest originally came from Witch Pongwiffy of the Witchway Wood Coven. A host of fabulous prizes awaits the lucky winners ...'

And Sheridan went on to explain about the fabulous prizes, while the Wizards paid close attention.

'... a silver trophy, a bag of gold, a recording contract with top producer Phil Spectre and a week's all-expenses-paid holiday in Sludgehaven-on-Sea. All of which will be presented –' Sheridan paused and smirked at the camera – '... by none other than myself. So, get that form filled in and sent off without delay.

'And now, sport. The hockey match between St Banshees and Harpy Girls High got off to a bad start when –'

The sound cut off, leaving Sheridan mouthing soundlessly like a stranded carp. Dave the Druid – a short, plump wizard with a big beard and half-glasses – stood before the screen, obviously keen to say something. There were a few protests.

'Turn it up!'

'Hey! I was watching that!'

Dave held up a hand.

'Did you hear that, gentlemen?' he asked. 'A Song Contest! What about that for an idea?'

'It's clever,' observed Gerald the Just, a hawk-nosed Wizard with a reputation for being fair. 'It gets everyone interested, there's the element of competition and the studio won't have to pay the performers because everyone wants to be on spellovision. Shame the Witches came up with the idea first. But it's clever. You have to hand it to them.'

'Let's hope they don't win as well,' came a voice from thin air. It belonged to Alf the Invisible, who was supposed to take reversing pills, but kept forgetting. 'That'll be something else they can throw in our faces.'

'They won't win. Not if I can help it,' declared Dave the Druid, eyes glinting with the light of battle. 'I don't know about you lot, but I reckon I can hold a tune. I come from the valleys, I do, and we're known for our singing. And it can't be *that* hard to come up with a song. If someone would have a bash at the words, I can set 'em to music. Any volunteers?'

A lone hand hesitantly rose and hovered in the air. The Wizards turned and stared at the owner.

The owner was the youngest Wizard there. His name was Ronald and he happened to be Sharkadder's nephew. Three disadvantages, and that's without even mentioning his spots. He went pink as everyone fell about laughing.

'Think of yourself as a bit of a wordsmith, do you, young fellow?' sneered Frank the Foreteller, who loved baiting Ronald.

'I'll give it a go, certainly,' said Ronald.

'Hm. Well, let's hope you come up with the goods. I've a feeling this Song Contest will be popular.'

He was right. The moment that the contest was announced, everyone wanted to be in it. Ali Pali could hardly open the studio door for entry forms.

The Trolls were into hard, heavy rock music. The hard, heavy rocks weren't a problem. The music bit was more difficult. Trolls aren't known for their singing talent. However, a youngster named Cliff Rigid had come up with some lyrics that sounded promising.

The Banshee Girls' Choir was entering a jolly

little ditty entitled 'Oh, Woe!' The Zombies were working on some sort of comedy number. Xotindis and Xstufitu, the two Mummies who lived in the Wood, were singing a duet. There was a rumour that a lone Werewolf named Roger would be entering a ballad or something. Four Vampires had formed a barbershop quartet. If you went for a walk in the woods at any time, day or night, you would hear snatches of song and bursts of drumming, twanging, scraping and honking issuing from caves, sheds, castles and underground holes.

The Familiars rehearsed in an old, ruined barn on the edge of the wood. You already know Hugo and Dudley. You have also met Snoop, Rory, Vernon, Steve and Barry. The others are: Speks (Greymatter's Owl); Bonidle's Sloth (who has no name because Bonidle can't be bothered to give him one); IdentiKit and CopiCat (twin Siamese cats belonging to the twins) and, last but not least, a large posse of Bats that hangs around Gaga.

They were gathered in the dimly lit barn. The Bats hung in a neat line from a shadowy rafter. Barry perched on the handle of an old rake. Vernon and Steve sat on a crate that had once held apples. IdentiKit and CopiCat had made themselves comfortable in a pile of straw. The Sloth was asleep on an ancient tarpaulin. Rory the Haggis was leaning against a rusty old plough. Filth the Fiend, Sludgegooey's Familiar, wasn't there because he was the drummer with the Witchway Rhythm Boys and already had a rehearsal.

Snoop was in a corner, cleaning his nails with his pitchfork, sulking because he wasn't in charge. It didn't seem right, bearing in mind that his mistress was the Grandwitch. However, although Snoop was a good organizer, his talents were sadly lacking in the musical department, and he had been elbowed to one side by Hugo, who was currently standing on a soap box, holding a tiny sheaf of papers in his paw.

'So what have ye got there, wee Hugo?' asked Rory.

'Is vords,' explained Hugo. 'Vords for our sonk. I hope you like.'

'I very much doubt *I* will,' muttered Speks, who, like his mistress, considered himself a bit of a poet. Greymatter was the intelligent Witch in the Witchway coven. Speks often helped her with the crossword. (*One Across. Night bird with a reputation for wisdom. Three letters, beginning with O and ending with L.* That sort of thing.)

'Give him a chance,' protested Vernon. 'You haven't heard it yet. Might be good.'

'Ar. An' fishes might use umbrellas,' sneered a

voice from the doorway. Dudley sauntered in, sat down and awarded Hugo a challenging glare.

Very sensibly, Hugo ignored him. He could fight Dudley any time. Right now, there was work to be done.

'Song is called "Oh I Do Like to Be a Vitch Familiar".'

'Sounds promising,' remarked Barry, politely.

'Sounds rubbish,' scoffed Dudley.

'Fire away, then, wee Hugo,' said Rory. 'Let's hear it.'

Hugo took a deep breath and burst into squeaky song.

> *'Oh, I do like to be a Vitch Familiar,*
> *I do like to help viz all ze spells.*
> *I don't even mind when zey go wrong, wrong, wrong,*
> *Causing a great big bang and a terrible pong, pong,*
>   *pong . . .'*

Yes. The Music Express had arrived in Witchway Wood all right, and everyone wanted to climb aboard.

CHAPTER FOURTEEN
Car Problems

Much to his annoyance, Sheridan Haggard was being stalked by Goblins. Or, to be precise, his car was. Everywhere he went, there they were, gathered in a silent little cluster, open-mouthed and staring. Quite often, he noticed, they were carrying stuff – a bath, an old chair, bits of assorted ironmongery.

Whenever he left the limo unattended, they would creep out from behind trees and surround it. The second his back was turned, there they would be, crouching down, poking at the wheels, pushing the windscreen wipers to and fro, playing with the mirror and, worst of all, laying their grubby hands on the paintwork!

'It's intolerable!' Sheridan raged to the Thing. 'The nerve! I won't put up with it, I tell you!'

Of course, Sheridan didn't know what lay behind the Goblins' disturbing behaviour. For the past few nights, they had been making regular raids on Pongwiffy's dump in order to collect items that fell under the general heading of Car Stuff.

They had had long discussions about the essential components that made up a car. So far, all they agreed on was wheels, seats, doors, windows and, of course, fluffy dice. And probably some other bits and bobs. Then they would join them all together. Somehow.

To their great dismay, *Goblins in Cars* was no longer on spello, so they didn't even have that as a reference any more. Examining Sheridan's limo just might give them some clues.

(The Goblins weren't the only ones who were fed up about losing *Goblins in Cars*. As we know, it was Macabre's favourite programme. When it got taken off, she had thrown a boot through the screen and vowed never to watch spello again.)

Funnily enough, people in general didn't seem to be watching spellovision so much these days. Making music seemed to be the current fad. Not that the Goblins cared *what* everyone else was into. Car assembly was their thing.

Anyway, Sheridan had a dilemma. He didn't want to stop using his limousine, which was one of the top perks of being a famous newsreader. But he didn't want it swarmed over by Goblins every time he left it unattended. He couldn't leave the Thing to mind it because who would open doors, pour champagne, fluff up his cushion, wipe his brow and sharpen his newsreading pencil?

In the end, he decided to try leaving Ribs to guard it. This would have worked fine if Ribs had had a guard-dog-type disposition. But he didn't. He was a mild, jolly little dog who liked everybody. Even Goblins.

The limousine was currently parked outside the spellovision studios where Sheridan was reading out the first news bulletin of the evening. The moment he disappeared inside, with the Thing hot on his heels, seven squat shapes crept from behind the bushes and clustered around the car. Ribs instantly perked up, stood on his hind legs and smiled toothily through the window, bony tail wagging like mad.

'Ah, look at him,' said Plugugly, staring through the glass, a soppy smile on his face. 'Dere's a good little doggy. Hello dere, little feller. Who's a nice little doggy den? Who's got a pretty sparkly collar? Coooeeee, doggy, doggy, doggy.'

'Wot, is there a dog in the car or summink?' asked

Lardo, who had been bending down, studying a tyre.

'Yes. He got a waggy tail, look!' Plugugly tapped on the glass. 'Hello, little doggy.'

'Woof,' said Ribs, jumping up and slobbering all over the window. Quite how he managed to slobber, considering he was made entirely of bones, is something of a mystery – but slobber he did.

'I *fink* I see where the smoke comes out,' shouted Hog, who was lying underneath the limousine, peering up at its underside. 'There's a pipe fing. I'll see if it's hot. *Ow, ow, ow, me finger!* Yes.'

'Can you see where it's comin' from, though?' Slopbucket wanted to know.

'No,' admitted Hog. 'It's too dark.'

'Well, we need to find that out, don't we?' said Eyesore. 'Cos it's the smoke what makes it go, I reckon.'

'Know what I reckon?' chipped in Stinkwart. 'I reckon there's a little horse in here. Under this bit.' He rapped on the gleaming bonnet.

'How's it make the smoke, though?' asked Eyesore.

'Perhaps it's smokin' a pipe,' said Stinkwart.

'Horses don't smoke pipes, do they?' enquired young Sproggit.

'Trained specially, I expect,' said Stinkwart,

113

unwilling to let the smoking–horse idea go. 'Trained to go an' stop and smoke a pipe.'

'It's a very quiet horse,' observed Slopbucket. 'You don't hear it neighin' or anythin'.'

'Or coughin',' added Lardo. 'It'd cough, wouldn't it? If it smoked a pipe. I don't reckon there's a horse in there at all. It's somethin' else makin' it go. A baby dragon, perhaps. What d'you reckon, Plug?'

But Plugugly wasn't paying attention. He was too taken with Ribs, who was now bouncing around on the back seat, crashing playfully into the window.

'Nice little doggy,' cooed Plugugly. 'Is oo hungry? Does oo want a bone?'

''E's got a bone,' remarked Sproggit. 'If 'e was that hungry, 'e could eat his own foot.' He gave a little snigger.

Just at that moment, there came an enraged cry. Sheridan had finished reading the news and had spotted them through the studio window, which overlooked the car park.

'Hey! You there! What have I told you? *Get away from my car!*'

'Oops,' said Slopbucket. 'Time to skidoodle.'

And with one accord, they took to their heels. Well, six of them did. Plugugly was still besotted with Ribs and didn't notice.

'Poor little doggy,' he was crooning, as Ribs

thrashed around, beside himself with excitement. 'Did dey leave oo on oo's ownio? Did dey? I wouldn't, not if you was mine. Dere, dere, never mind . . .'

He broke off as he found his arms gripped firmly by Hog and Lardo, and was dragged off into the night.

Abandoned, Ribs gave a sad little whimper as his new friend was borne away. Without much hope, he launched himself at the window one last time. His bony back leg landed accidentally on the door handle. There was a click and, to his surprise, the heavy door swung open.

Freedom!

With a happy little woof, Ribs jumped out and merrily scampered off in pursuit of Plugugly.

The moonlight streamed in as the Goblins rolled the boulder to one side and squeezed into the cave. There wasn't much room, because of all the Car Stuff. It rose in a vast, teetering pile, slap bang in the middle.

Do you want to know what there was? I'll tell you.

One broken cartwheel. One old pram. One supermarket trolley. Two nude deckchairs (i.e. no cloth, frame only). One rotten garden bench. Four broken kitchen stools. One overstuffed armchair with a spring sticking up through the seat. A bundle of forks. A roll of garden wire. String. A box of candles. A collection of rusty saucepans. One large tin of turquoise paint. One collapsed umbrella. Three bottomless buckets. A set of taps, both hot and cold. The grill off a camping stove. A broken anglepoise lamp. One parrot cage. One large tin bath. One mangle . . .

No. I can't bear it any more. Imagine it for yourselves.

'Here we all are, then,' said Stinkwart. ''Ome again. Back to the pile.'

'We got enough stuff now, ain't we?' asked Sproggit. 'Ain't it time we started?'

'Yeah!' came the united chorus. 'Yeah! Let's make the car! Let's make the car! Let's make . . .'

'All right,' agreed Plugugly. He sounded a bit reluctant, though. 'We'll start. Even dough I is still feelin' sad an' not at my best. Don't fink I has forgiven you for pullin' me away from dat little doggy. I liked dat little doggy, I did. I wish I had a little doggy of my own.'

'You'll like 'avin' a car though, won'tcha?' soothed Stinkwart. 'Come on. You know you will.'

'True,' agreed Plugugly, cheering up. Rolling up his shirtsleeves, he stepped towards the huge junk

116

mountain that soared up into the shadows and spat on his palms. 'You is quite right, Stinkwart, I *will* like dat. So what is we waitin' for? Come on, boys! Let's make a car!'

CHAPTER FIFTEEN
The Song

Over now to Witchway Hall. Pongwiffy and Sharkadder are about to unleash their lovely new song on the Coven and we don't want to miss that, do we? We know how hard they've been working on it.

'I'm feeling a bit nervous, aren't you?' whispered Sharkadder, applying a fresh coat of prune lipstick with a shaky hand. 'How do I look?'

'Fine,' mumbled Pongwiffy, without looking. To tell the truth, she was feeling a bit queasy. They were running late because Sharkadder kept changing her mind about what to wear – plus, they had had a lot to carry. So Pongwiffy had used one of her unreliable transportation spells, which got them there in double-quick time but left their tummies lagging three minutes behind in the process.

The Coven was all ready and waiting. Excitement was in the air. Witches like nothing better than the opportunity to criticize.

'I must say I'm looking forward to this,' remarked Bendyshanks to Ratsnappy as the composers took their seats and nervously organized themselves with music stands, guitar, harmonica, glasses of water, thermos, emergency sandwiches, throat sweets and lyrics, copied on to a sheet of paper in Sharkadder's neat hand. 'I wonder what they've come up with. If it's awful, let's boo.'

'I hope it's a nice ballad,' said Sludgegooey. 'I love a nice, romantic ballad, me.'

'Ballad!' scoffed Macabre, overhearing. 'We dinnae need that cissy stuff. We need somethin' dark an' dramatic, wi' words that reflect the true Witch experience. Damp caves an' blasted heaths an' cauldrons full o' heavin' murk.'

'But only Witches would like that, wouldn't they? We need a song that'll appeal to everyone, don't we?' mused Scrofula. She raised her voice and shouted, 'What's it called, Pongwiffy?'

'"Banga Langa Bing Bong Boo",' said Pongwiffy and Sharkadder together. There were a few raised eyebrows at this, and a certain amount of muttering.

'Why?' asked Greymatter politely.

'Why not?' said Pongwiffy, plucking a string and fiddling with a peg as though she knew what she was doing.

'Let's save the questions for later, shall we?' said Sharkadder briskly. 'Trust us, Greymatter, we know what we're doing. We've been writing songs together for ages now, haven't we, Pong?'

'Oh yes,' said Pongwiffy. 'We're very experienced.' And she swept her hand over the strings. *Thruuuuuuuummmmmm.* 'Right. That's me tuned up.'

'Get a move on, then,' said Sourmuddle, who was sitting at the piano with her arms folded. 'Let's hear it. I hope it's good. We want to win this contest.'

'On my count, Sharky,' said Pongwiffy. 'One, two, three!'

And together, over Pongwiffy's horrible thrumming, they burst into song.

'Well, here's a little ditty
We're sure you'll want to sing.
It isn't very witty
And it doesn't mean a thing,
But we know you're gonna love it,
Of that we have no doubt,
Cos once it's lodged inside your head
You'll never get it out!

120

Oooooooooooh . . .
Banga-langa binga-linga bonga-longa, bing, bong, boo,
Rooti-tooti, that's a beauty, rama-dama ding, dong, do,
Twiddle-twaddle, nod your noddle, see if you can do it too,
Banga-langa binga-linga bonga-longa bing, bong, boo!'

Pongwiffy played her discord one last time, Sharkadder gave her harmonica a long, vigorous suck, then there was silence. A long, long silence.

'So what do you think?' asked Pongwiffy, hopefully.

More silence.

'Would you like to hear it again?' offered Pongwiffy.

All eyes were on Sourmuddle, who was sitting with her head on one side and her eyes closed. She was the Grandwitch. Nobody liked to venture an opinion until she had spoken. Suddenly, she opened her eyes, gave a brisk little nod and said, 'It'll do.'

'She likes it!' shrieked Pongwiffy.

'She likes it!' trilled Sharkadder. They both leapt to their feet, linked arms and did a celebratory little jig.

'I'm not saying it's great music, mind,' added Sourmuddle. 'In fact, musically speaking, it's rubbish. But it's rubbish with universal appeal. The sort of thing people hum in the bath. Am I right?'

It didn't do to disagree with Sourmuddle. With

one accord, everyone else decided that they liked it too.

'It's catchy, I'll say that,' agreed Scrofula.

'Aye. It wasnae what ah was expectin', but ah haveta say ah'm pleasantly surprised,' nodded Macabre.

'Sing it again,' ordered Sourmuddle. 'Without the harmonica solo this time. Pongwiffy, don't thrum so much.'

'I like to thrum,' said Pongwiffy, hurt. 'It's what I do.'

'Well, do it quieter,' ordered Sourmuddle.

So Pongwiffy and Sharkadder sang it again. And again. By the third time, everybody knew the words and was singing along. Even Bonidle roused herself enough to clap along and Gaga started dancing on the piano until Sourmuddle made her stop. There followed a noisy, cacophonous hour while those with instruments tried to work out what they would play and the singers practised getting the tune right. Then they tried it again.

And again.

And again.

Tell you what, let's leave them until they've got it sorted out. It's not much fun listening to people practise.

Instead, we'll go and find out how the Goblins are getting on.

CHAPTER SIXTEEN
'How Do Dey Make Cars Anyway?'

Badly, that's how. Goblins are just not practically minded. They have trouble doing up their own boot-laces, so it isn't surprising that building a car from scratch was proving a tad challenging.

Right now, most of them were gathered worriedly around the huge pile of junk, scratching their heads and talking about wheels. The problem wasn't how many were needed. They had already agreed on that. One on each corner and a spare on the back. Seven. Easy. No, the problem was that the wheels they had collected didn't match. They had: one cartwheel (broken), three pram wheels (two bent, one buckled) and four silly little ones from the old supermarket trolley.

'Car wheels are s'posed to look the same, ain't they?' said Slopbucket. 'You can't 'ave 'em different sizes. It won't work, will it?'

'They ain't even proper car wheels,' said Eyesore. 'They'll look funny.'

'And another thing. What do we fix 'em to?' fretted Eyesore. 'We gotta join 'em on to the bit we sit in. And we 'aven't decided what that's gonna be, 'ave we?'

'The bath,' said Hog. 'It's gotta be. It's the only fing big enough.'

'Here!' said Lardo suddenly, clapping a hand to his head. 'Where's my hat?'

'Who cares? I'm bored. Why can't we stop talkin'?' whined young Sproggit.

'What about the seats, though?' said Stinkwart, ignoring them both. 'There's gotta be *seats,* right? We agreed.'

'Oh yeah,' concurred Hog. 'You never see a car wivout seats.'

'It's gone, ain't it?' cried Lardo, all panicky. 'I've lost it, 'aven't I? I've lost my hat!"

'Let's start,' whinged Sproggit. 'There's too much talkin'. I wanna start.'

'These ain't proper car seats, though, are they?' said Eyesore to Stinkwart, Slopbucket and Hog. 'They won't fit in the bath, will they?'

They cast uneasy eyes over the motley array of seats. Two deckchair frames, a sagging garden bench, four dilapidated stools and a large armchair. Lardo had lost interest and was running round in circles, looking for his missing hat.

'They'd fit if we chopped 'em up,' suggested Stinkwart.

'But then they're not *seats*, are they?' pointed out Hog. 'What we got then is a bath full o' wood.'

'Sit on that an' we'll get splinters in our bums,' observed Sproggit, grinning.

Loud guffaws erupted at this. Any mention of bums is guaranteed to send Goblins into fits of uncontrollable laughter.

'Ha ha!' they roared. 'Bum! 'Ear that? Oh ha ha ha!'

Lardo didn't join in. He was too upset about his hat. Neither did Plugugly, who was sitting a little way apart. He had given himself the task of making the fiddly bits. Right now, he was hopelessly wondering how to make a car horn out of a garden hose, a piece of string and a lemon grater.

'Oi, Plug?' sniggered Sproggit. 'I said bum. 'Ear me? Tee hee.'

The Goblins collapsed anew with mirth.

'I heard,' sighed Plugugly. He had so hoped that, somewhere along the line, inspiration would come and the way forward would miraculously become clear. But it hadn't.

'So why ain't you laughin'?'

'Cos,' said Plugugly, 'cos dis is *serious*. Dis isn't a game we is havin'. Car buildin' is *serious*, right? We gone to all dat trouble gettin' all dis stuff an' tryin' to look at how cars is fitted togedder an' now we has got to de hard bit an' if we don't stop messin' about an' – an' *pull togedder* an' work out how to do it, we has wasted our time. I can't do it by myself. We has *all* got to do it. Right?'

This was probably the longest, most solemn speech he had made in his entire life. The rest of the Gaggle listened to it with respectful incomprehension.

'Right,' said Sproggit. 'Still – *bum*,' he added, with a little snort, setting the Goblins off again.

Plugugly looked at them writhing around helplessly. Then he looked at the huge pile of junk. Briefly, he closed his eyes, and the vision came to him. The vision that haunted his dreams. The one where he was bowling along a road at the wheel of a shiny limousine, the twin of Sheridan Haggard's, *exactly* like it except just a fraction bigger, with the sun shining and the windows open. Off to the seaside, with a posh picnic in the boot. Wayfarers pointing and crying out with amazement as he passed ...

He opened his eyes. Lardo was looking down his own trousers for his hat. Hog had climbed on to the seat of the armchair and was bouncing up and down, making chicken noises. Sproggit was poking Stinkwart with the collapsed umbrella and Eyesore and Slopbucket had placed buckets over their heads and were charging each other head first.

Why had he ever thought it would work? Why?

'I dunno,' he said sadly. 'How do dey make cars anyway?'

Nobody even heard.

He heaved a deep sigh, threw down the hose and the string, kicked the lemon grater into a corner and walked out of the cave.

Outside, just to bring him down even more, as well as getting dark it was damp. A thin, depressing drizzle was slowly turning the scrubby slopes of the Lower Misty Mountains into a mudslide.

Plugugly turned up his collar, thrust his hands into his pockets and trudged off down the slope. He needed to be alone for a while, to get over his disappointment. Actually, he wasn't sure he would *ever* get over it.

Why did things never work out right for Goblins? Why did other people get all the brains and all the luck? Why was it always *somebody else* who found a mysterious ring or Magic lamp or lucky stone or something and got three wishes? Why? Why, for instance, couldn't he have a pet, like that nice little dog? At least it would be company. And he could take it for walks and train it to bite Sproggit, who was really getting on his nerves these days.

He aimed a dejected kick at a small pebble lying in his path.

And that's when he heard it. A jolly little sound, coming from somewhere off in the distance.

'*Woof!*'

Plugugly stopped. Had he imagined it?

'*Woof! Woof!*' No. It was coming closer. Could it be?

He rounded a clump of prickly bushes – and suddenly his arms were full of wagging, wiggling bones!

'Doggy!' cried Plugugly, drowning in happiness and slobber. 'My little doggy!'

'Faster!' instructed Sheridan Haggard. 'Faster, *faster*! Put your foot down!'

'I am,' said the Thing, screeching around a corner on two wheels. 'It's a bendy road, boss. Calm down, why doncha?'

'Calm *down*?' boomed Sheridan, all righteous indignation. 'A pack of Goblins have stolen my beloved pet and you're telling me to *calm down*?'

'You don't *know* they stole 'im, though, do you? You didn't see 'em actually do it.'

'Of course they did it! They were messing around with the limo again, I saw them!'

'Yeah, but the doors was locked, I know cos I did it meself. Ribs musta opened it 'imself, from the inside.'

'He's a *dog*, Thing, not a locksmith or a-a-a trained octopus! No, it's quite clear what happened. Those wretched Goblins managed to force the door open and they've stolen him for his lovely jewelled collar. Oh, Ribsy, my poor little Ribsy! Why did I leave you?'

Sheridan began to sob. Large tears trickled down his smooth cheekbones. (This may surprise you. But then, Ribs can slobber and both of them can eat and drink. Skeletons have their own mysterious ways of doing things, and that's that.)

'Hold tight, boss!' advised the Thing, crashing the gears and narrowly avoiding a rock. 'We're goin' up the mountain. Lot o' potholes. One comin' up right n–'

As he spoke, there came the unmistakable sound of a skull crashing into a hard roof, followed by a very rude, un-newsreader-like word.

'Oops,' said the Thing. 'See what I mean?'

★

Up in the cave, it suddenly dawned on the Goblins that Plugugly was missing.

'Where's he gone?' asked Hog.

'Who cares?' sniffed Lardo. He was down in the dumps because he still hadn't found his hat. The others shrugged their shoulders and looked blank.

'When did we see him last?' pondered Hog. 'Anyone remember?'

''E was makin' that speech,' said Stinkwart. 'About bein' serious about somethin'. 'E sounded a bit fed up. I didn't take it seriously, though.'

'*He's* fed up?' sulked Lardo. 'Huh. At least he ain't lost 'is hat.'

'Think we should go and look for 'im?' (Hog)

'Why?' (Sproggit)

'I dunno. We're s'posed to be makin' the car, right? It was his idea. Why should we do all the work while he slopes off?'

'Oh. Right!'

So the six of them set off to look for Plugugly. Slipping and sliding down the muddy slope, they were soon swallowed up by shadows.

No sooner had they vanished than two headlights stabbed the darkness and Sheridan's sleek limousine came purring up the track, coming to a halt directly outside the Goblin cave.

The driver's door shot open and the Thing scrambled out, pausing only to dispose of his chauffeur hat and don a pair of minder-type dark glasses to make him look tough before racing round to open the passenger door in the back. After a brief pause, Sheridan emerged. He unfolded his bony frame with a series of little clicks and pops, then stared around grimly in the fading light, taking in the depressing surroundings.

'Ribs?' he shouted. 'Are you there, boy?'

Silence. Without another word, Sheridan stalked towards the cave with the Thing hurrying at his heels.

Rather to their surprise, the front boulder was rolled to one side. Beyond lay total darkness. Sheridan bent down and squinted in.

'Hello there!' he called, his golden-brown voice bouncing off the walls. 'Anybody in?'

Silence.

'There's no point in hiding, you know,' boomed Sheridan, threateningly. 'I know you're in there. Send out the dog, then come out yourselves with your hands up. I'm making a Skeleton's arrest. I shall count to three.'

More silence.

'One – two – three! That's it, I'm coming in!'

'Hang on, boss. Could be a trap,' advised the Thing, in his role as bodyguard.

'Oh. Do you really think so?'

'Could be.'

'In that case, you go first.'

'Right,' said the Thing stoutly. 'Here I go. Stay right there.'

And he marched into the cave.

'What can you see?' called Sheridan.

'Nuffin',' shouted the Thing. 'I'm feelin' me way round the edges.'

'Is it safe?'

'Well, I don't fink there's anyone home.'

'In that case, I'm coming in. Wow! It's very dark. I can't see a thing ...'

A cave in total darkness is hazardous enough, what with low bits of ceiling to bang your head on and half-buried rocks to trip over. It is made doubly dangerous when it contains a huge, tottering, precariously balanced mountain of rubbish.

As you might expect, Sheridan walked slap bang into it!

If you had been standing outside, you would have heard a startled cry – then a rumbling, slithering effect, followed by dramatic crashing and tinkling noises as the huge edifice came tumbling down.

Then silence.

★

'An' dat's when I found de Lucky Wishin' Pebble,' gabbled Plugugly happily as the Gaggle hurried back up the slope with Ribs racing around their ankles. 'Just as I was rememberin' about de little dog and wishin' he was mine. An' I kicked it, just like dat, an' den suddenly, dere 'e was! De little dog, wot I love. Just as I was feelin' sad about de car an' wishin' sumfin' good would happen. An' den I kicked it again an' wished I 'ad someone to tell about it an' you lot shows up! Den I kicked it again!'

'An' what happened?'

'Well – nuffin. But at least I got a new doggy.'

'I wants to borrow the Lucky Wishin' Pebble,' whined Lardo. 'I wants me hat back.'

'I fink it only works for me,' Plugugly told him sadly. 'Sorry.'

'What we gonna call the doggy?' asked Slopbucket. 'Needs a name, don't 'e? What's a good name fer a dog?'

'Puss?' suggested Hog.

'Fluffy?' (That was Stinkwart's offering.)

'Mr Stuart Prichard?' (Sproggit, being particularly weird.)

'Who?' said everybody, staring at him.

'Mr Stuart Prichard. That's the name of my gran's dentist.'

'Well, it's not a good name for a little doggy,' said

Plugugly firmly. 'If you fink I'm gonna call my little doggy Mr Stuart Prichard, you is mad. No, I know what I is gonna call him. I is gonna call him Fang de Wonder Hound. I is gonna teach him tricks an' everyfin'. Now, if only we had a car, everyfin' would be jus' perfect – *Hold it!*'

He came to sudden stop. Everyone piled up behind, like dominoes. Fang the Wonder Hound stopped racing around like a mad thing and came to sit at Plugugly's feet, panting up lovingly into his face. For once, Plugugly didn't notice. Something had caught his attention.

'Look!' he gasped, pointing with a trembling hand. 'De Lucky Pebble *did* work anudder time after all!'

Sure enough, there, outside the cave, stood the car of their dreams. Fang the Wonder Hound recognized it immediately, and proceeded to bite the tyres.

'It's exackly like the uvver one!' marvelled Hog. 'The one that Skellington's got. Same colour, everyfin'! That's some Pebble you got there, Plug.'

'I know,' said Plugugly, proudly. He fingered the wonderful stone deep in his pocket, reached down and gave his new pet a fierce, loving hug. For once, all his dreams were coming true.

Hardly daring to believe their own eyes, the Goblins crept forward and ran their hands over the limousine's gleaming surface. Experimentally, Eyesore pressed the handle on the driver's door. Instantly, it swung open, revealing a rich, leather interior and a set of keys hanging from the ignition.

'It's open!' breathed Hog.

'So what are we waitin' for?' squealed Sproggit, wild with excitement. 'Let's go for a drive! Let's go on holiday! Right *now*!'

There was a sudden silence.

'Can we drive?' asked Eyesore doubtfully.

'No,' came the chorus.

'Do we care?'

'No!'

'Then let's go!'

Overcome with emotion, young Sproggit threw his hat in the air, sank to his knees in the dirt and hugged the fender.

'Best push the boulder over,' said Slopbucket. 'Don't wanna come 'ome an' find we bin robbed.'

'Right,' said Hog. 'They might nick our stuff.'

'We ain't got any stuff,' observed Lardo. 'Except our huntin' bags. And they got holes in.'

'What about the Car Stuff?' Eyesore said.

'We don't need that now we got a proper car, though, do we?' said Stinkwart.

'Eyesore is right,' said Plugugly. 'We doesn't want people snoopin' about. Supposin' someone tells

Pongwiffy? We'll be for it. Or what if a bear comes along lookin' for somewhere to move in?'

Everyone agreed that it made sense to roll the boulder back in place. Nobody thought to check inside first, of course. That's Goblins for you.

CHAPTER SEVENTEEN

Robbed!

'I don't believe it!' wailed Pongwiffy. 'I've been robbed!'

She was standing, looking out over the rubbish tip with Sharkadder. It was a bright, sunny morning – the first morning she had seen for some time. Nights had been taken up with rehearsals and the days spent catching up with eating, sleeping and shouting at Hugo.

'It's a bit depleted, I'll give you that,' agreed Sharkadder.

'Depleted? It's a shadow of its former self! Stripped bare of all the choice bits! The bath, the mangle, the shopping trolley – gone, all gone!'

'We're talking about a rubbish tip here, Pong,'

remarked Sharkadder. 'I don't know why you're getting quite so worked up.'

'Because it's *my* rubbish tip. Mine. I've been so busy lately I just haven't thought to check on it. And somebody's been here helping themselves while my back's been turned. Who, I wonder. Who'd be stupid enough to tangle with me?'

'Actually, I think I can help you there,' said Sharkadder. She stooped down and poked a long green talon at something lying by her boot. 'Look. A clue.' Gingerly, she picked up the grubby item and held it out. 'A Goblin hat, if I'm not very much mistaken.'

'Typical!' raged Pongwiffy. 'Sneaky little tea leaves! How dare they? Well, they'll be sorry. Just wait till I get my hands on 'em. In fact, I'll do it right now, while the mood's on me. I'll just go and get my wand. Coming?'

'No,' said Sharkadder, adding, 'and neither are you. Now is not the time, Pong. We've got to focus on the Contest. Just think, tomorrow night! Only thirty-six hours to go. And I haven't even started putting my make-up on.'

'Gosh,' said Pongwiffy, startled. 'Is it? Is it *really* tomorrow?'

'Yes. Isn't it terrifying? In a sort of deliciously exciting way? I simply can't wait to see myself on

138

spello. I can't decide what to wear. Lilac or puce? Shoes or boots? Hat or no hat? Whenever I think of it, I come over all of a flutter. I just know our song will win, don't you?'

'Sure to,' agreed Pongwiffy, adding, 'although I've got a feeling the Familiars'll be strong contenders. Hugo's very competitive. And they say the Banshees are good. And then there are the Wizards. You know how they like to get one over on us . . .'

'Oh, stop being doomy!' cried Sharkadder gaily. 'Have faith! Of course we'll win, with our brilliant song.'

'You're right,' said Pongwiffy, cheering up. 'It *is* a good song, isn't it?'

'It's perfect. We'll win, and then we'll get presented with the cup and I'll be on spello and get to meet Sheridan Haggard and we'll get a lovely holiday and – Oh, I'm so excited I could *burst*! I do think a Spellovision Song Contest is one of your best ever ideas, Pong, I really do! Come on – let's go and practise!'

'All right,' said Pongwiffy. 'But those Goblins are really for it when I catch up with them.'

Ali Pali sat in his office with his feet on his desk, smoking a big cigar and studying the latest viewing figures. There was good news and bad news.

The bad news was that the viewing public was getting fussier by the hour. No longer could people be palmed off with a load of cheap Gnomes. In fact, Gnomes were currently out of favour. Anything featuring Gnomes caused people to switch off in droves. People didn't seem to be interested in Fiends much, either, or in celebrity Dwarf chefs, or in instructive documentaries about embalming.

The only programme that continued to enjoy undiminished popularity was *The News*. People always tuned in for that. It had become even more popular since the announcement about the forthcoming Spellovision Song Contest. Every news bulletin ended with Sheridan reading out the latest entrants.

The Spellovision Song Contest. Here, at last, was good news. Oh yes. Very good news indeed.

These days, the talk was of nothing else. In Witch cottages, Troll caves and Ghost haunted castles, the excited contestants would switch on *The News*, then sit on the edge of their seats in great excitement, waiting for their own name to be read out in Sheridan's rich, honeyed tones. When it came, they would go pink and either nudge their fellow watchers or hug themselves, if they were alone.

Pongwiffy's Hamster had been right. A Spellovision Song Contest was a magnificent idea. It held universal appeal. Spellovisions were selling like hot cakes. Desperate advertisers were sending bundles of used notes through the post in the hopes of bribing Ali Pali to show their advertisement at peak time, when the whole world would be watching.

Ali hoped he was going to make a *lot* of money.

CHAPTER EIGHTEEN

Trapped!

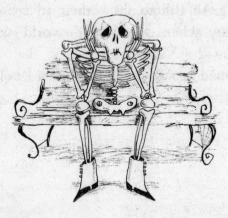

Sheridan Haggard sat on the rotten garden bench, skull in hands, attempting to recover from his ordeal. It had taken ages for the Thing to dig him out from beneath the avalanche of rubbish. He still felt shaky.

'Feelin' better now, boss?' enquired the Thing. It was of a practical disposition, was the Thing, and possessed of exceptional energy, which is why it made such a good Everything Else Boy. It also possessed a useful box of matches. As well as extracting both itself and Sheridan from the sea of junk, it had located a couple of candle stubs stuck in niches in the walls, so at least they were no longer in darkness. It was now scuttling about tidying up – a thankless task owing to the sheer volume of rubbish, but, then again, the Thing specialized in thankless tasks.

'I feel *terrible*,' groaned Sheridan. 'I'm covered in filth, my skull aches and I'm suffering from shock. Quick! Champagne! Failing that, mineral water.'

'No water here, boss,' said the Thing cheerfully. 'I've checked. No grub either.'

'In that case,' said Sheridan, attempting to rise in a wobbly way, then sitting back down again, 'I shall leave immediately. Assist me to my feet and help me outside. I require fresh air.'

'Can't be done, boss,' said the Thing. It pointed to the heavy boulder that blocked the opening. 'See? Someone's stuck the stone back. We can't get out. You'd need a lot o' muscle power to shift that baby.'

Whistling cheerily, it waded around in the sea of rubbish, collecting up armfuls of miscellaneous tat, totally unfazed by their grim situation.

'Are you telling me,' began Sheridan, voice trembling with indignation, 'are you *seriously* telling me that we are *stuck here*? Without food and drink? In a *Goblin cave* that for some mysterious reason contains the world's biggest scrap heap, which has recently *collapsed on my head*?'

'Yep.'

'But – this is *preposterous*! How did that boulder get there?'

'Someone pushed it, I s'pose,' said the Thing with a shrug.

'Who?'

'Didn't see, did I? I was pulling you out from under the junk at the time. But whoever did it took the limo. I heard it leave.'

'The limo?' Sheridan, white already, went even whiter with shock. 'They've taken *my limo*?'

''Fraid so.'

'Well, I'm not having it!' announced Sheridan. He rose to his feet, swayed a bit, then tottered over to the cave mouth. He set his shoulder bone to the boulder and pushed with all his might. His slight weight made no impression whatsoever.

'Give up, boss,' said the Thing. 'You're too flimsy. You'll do yourself an injury.'

Sheridan strained ineffectually for another few seconds, then gave in. Gasping, he staggered back to the bench, buried his skull in his hands again and groaned with despair.

'Cheer up,' advised the Thing. 'It could be worse.'

'How?' moaned Sheridan in hollow tones.

'Well, at least we got matches an' there's plenty o' chair legs an' that. We can light a fire if we gets cold.'

'Oh yes,' said Sheridan, heavily sarcastic. 'That's a *good* idea. Let's start a *big fire* in a *cave we can't get out of.* Oh, what *fun,* do *let's.*'

'All right,' said the Thing, a bit sniffily. 'No need to be sarky.'

'There is *every* need!' shouted Sheridan. His golden voice had acquired a tinny, not-so-golden edge. 'Don't you realize how serious this is? I am *the newsreader*! In less than one hour I am meant to be at my desk reading the midnight bulletin! Not trapped in a stinking Goblin cave drowning in tin trays and old prams, watching you *tidy up* like some kind of demented Cinderella!'

'I can't help it,' argued the Thing. 'I gotta keep busy. It's me nature.'

'Well, I forbid it! Stop it this instant and think of a plan to get us out of here! Make it quick. I've never liked small spaces. Come on, come on! I'm already going stir crazy! Arggh! The walls, the walls! *The walls are closing in!*'

Sheridan reached out and clutched the Thing in a panicky grip.

'Calm down, boss! Take deep breaths!' advised the Thing, smacking at the bony hands.

'Get me out! Get me out!' howled Sheridan, breaking into a cold sweat. He stumbled over to the walls and began feeling them for cracks.

'I can't, boss. There ain't no way out. All we can do is wait until they send out a search party.'

Sheridan suddenly stood stock-still. There was a glimmer of hope in his eye sockets.

'Ah,' he said. 'A rescue party. Of course. They'll be sure to come looking when I don't turn up, right?'

'Sure to. You bein' such an important person an' all. See? Now you're thinkin' on the bright side.'

'Yes,' said Sheridan. He took out a large white hanky and mopped his streaming brow. 'Yes, you're quite right, Thing. I mustn't overreact. They'll send out a search party. There's one on its way right now, right?'

'Right,' soothed the Thing. 'And as soon as we hear 'em comin' we'll yell out an' they'll rescue us. Before you know it, you'll be reading out all about yerself on the news. It'll be in the paper too, I shouldn't wonder. Think of the publicity. *Famous Celebrity Newsreader Goblin Cave Rescue Drama*. I can see the headlines now.'

'Yes,' muttered Sheridan. He was calmer now, but still a bit twitchy. 'Yes, you're right. Of course. In fact, this is probably quite a good career move. But what about poor Ribs? We still haven't found him, have we?'

'He'll be all right. Probably found his own way 'ome by now. That, or gone wild and livin' with wolves.'

146

'I suppose you're right,' sighed Sheridan.

'I know I am. There. Feelin' better now?'

'A little.'

'So can I get on with the tidyin'?'

'*No!* Leave it, d'you hear? You take your orders from me. And right now, your job is to keep me amused. Take my mind off things. Entertain me until the rescue party arrives.'

'All right,' agreed the Thing, amiably. 'What do you want? I Spy? Charades? Fancy a sing song?'

'Oh, *bother*!' cried Sheridan, curling one hand into a bony fist and smacking it into the other. 'What did you have to say *that* for?'

'What? What did I say?'

'*Sing*. Now you've gone and reminded me that it's the Spellovision Song Contest tomorrow night and I'm presenting the trophy to the winner! I simply *have* to be there. I say! You don't think there's the slightest chance that we'll still be here tomorrow, do you?'

'No,' said the Thing, crossing its fingers behind its back.

'Tell the truth. I can take it.'

'Yes, then.'

'Aaargh!' wailed Sheridan. 'I can't take it! I can't! The walls are moving in again! The walls! *Stop the walls!*'

'I'm kiddin', I'm kiddin'! Calm down, all right? Course they'll find us. Any minute now, I expect. Tell you what. Sit down and I'll read to ya. 'Ow's that?'

'Read what? We haven't got any books.'

'That's what you think.' The Thing reached into its pocket, withdrew something the size of a matchbox and waved it triumphantly. 'See? A book. Found it amongst all the rubbish.'

'Really? What's it called?'

'*The Little Book of Hamster Wit and Wisdom*,' read the Thing, squinting at the tiny writing.

'Hmm. Odd sort of thing to turn up in a Goblins' cave. Still. I suppose it's better than nothing. Fire away.'

'Right. Shouldn't take long, it's very small. Are you sitting comfortably? Then I'll begin. *What kind of Hamsters live at the North Pole? Cold ones.* Ha, ha, get it? That's good, that is. Here's another one. *If at first you don't suck seed, suck, suck, suck again . . .*'

CHAPTER NINETEEN

Setting Up

The Spellovision Song Contest was going to be held in Witchway Hall. It was the only place big enough to hold the huge number of contestants taking part and their armies of supporters. (The Hall might not look like much from the outside, but the interior has the useful design feature of being able to Magically expand into the fourth dimension. When necessary, it can accommodate vast crowds.)

Vast crowds were what Ali Pali confidently expected. Vast crowds and record-breaking viewing figures.

Right now, he sat by himself in the front row, tapping numbers into his calculator whilst simultaneously smoking a big cigar and keeping an eye on the camera crew, which was busy setting up.

Everything was going to plan. The Tree Demon was scuttling about with a big furry microphone on a stick. Vincent Van Ghoul was ducking and bobbing around the aisles, staring through the viewfinder of his spellovision camera, trying out different angles. Brenda was directing a couple of cheap Gnomes where to put the scoreboard. The Witchway Rhythm Boys were in the orchestra pit, setting out their music stands.

There was only one niggling worry. Sheridan Haggard and the Everything Else Boy had gone missing. Nothing had been seen or heard of them since the evening news bulletin the night before. They hadn't turned up for the midnight news, which was highly unusual.

Ali had rung Sheridan's crystal ball to demand an explanation – but Sheridan wasn't answering. Ali had sent a runner round to Sinister Towers. The runner – a cheap Gnome – had come back saying that the castle was all locked up and the limo gone from the garage. No note of apology, no sign of foul play, nothing.

'Any news, boss?' asked Vincent Van Ghoul, squinting through his camera.

'No,' said Ali. 'Nothing.'

'I shouldn't worry,' said Vincent. 'He'll turn up. Catch Sheridan missing something like this. He's probably at the tailor's having a posh suit made for the occasion.'

'You may be right,' said Ali Pali. 'But I'm a businessman. I can't afford to take chances. This contest must go off without a hitch. Everything is riding on it. My reputation, as well as my bank balance.'

'Then you'll be pleased to know I've got it all under control,' broke in a new voice. An all too familiar odour was in the air. Ali Pali whirled round, startled. Pongwiffy was sitting in the seat directly behind him.

'Oh,' said Ali. 'It's you. What do you mean, under control?'

'Meaning,' said Pongwiffy smugly, 'meaning that I've written to my very good friend Scott Sinister, telling him to come along to present the prizes.'

'Really?' Ali Pali's beam went from ear to ear. 'But this is wonderful news! He's really coming?'

'Oh yes,' said Pongwiffy. 'He'll come all right. In fact, he'll be delighted.'

Actually, this wasn't quite true. Scott Sinister was less than delighted when Pongwiffy's missive dropped through the letterbox of his luxury trailer. It said:

deer scott,

i no you will be pleezed to hear frum me agin. yes, it is i, pongwiffy, yore number wun fan. hav you seen this new spellellovishun lark they got now? persnally i reckon it needs livening up. it is mi idea to haf a song contest wich i no evrywun wil enjoi espeshully as you are presentin the priz to the winers who will of cors be us witches. congratulashuns on reseeving this onour.

see you in witchway hawl nex saterday nite.

yore frend and admirer

pongwiffy

X X X X X

ps I dont trust that skellington who is renting yore cassel. shifty eye sockets.

CHAPTER TWENTY
The Contest Begins

The lights dimmed. Filth the Fiend played a drum roll. The audience settled back into their seats as a magnified voice boomed forth from nowhere.

'Ladies and gentlemen, viewers at home, welcome to the Witchway Wood Spellovision Song Contest! Please give a big hand to the head of Spellovision Enterprises and your host for this evening – the genial Genie, *Mr Ali Pali*!'

The Witchway Rhythm Boys launched into something jaunty, the lights came back up and the audience cheered wildly as Ali, plump paunch tightly encased in a glittery jacket, came running onstage, waving and smiling. He jogged to a halt by a large board on which was written the names of all the contestants placed alphabetically, like this:

Contestant	Song	Score
1. Banshees	'Oh Woe!'	☐
2. Familiars	'Oh, I Do Like to Be a Witch Familiar'	☐
3. Ghosts	'A Haunting We Will Go'	☐
4. Ghouls	'All the Nice Ghouls Love a Sailor'	☐
5. Gnomes	'Gnome, Sweet Gnome'	☐
6. Mummies	'All Wrapped Up and No Place to Go'	☐
7. Trolls	'We Will Rock You'	☐
8. Vampires	'That's a Very Nice Neck, By Heck! '	☐
9. Werewolf	'A Change is Gonna Come'	☐
10. Witches	'Banga Langa Bing Bong Boo!'	☐
11. Wizards	'The Long and Winding Beard'	☐
12. Zombies	'Whoops, There Goes Me Arm'	☐

Vincent Van Ghoul moved in for a close-up. Ali, smiling a dazzling smile that would have given a piano keyboard a run for its money, waited for the applause to subside, then said, 'Thank you, one and all. Well, what a wonderful occasion this is. First, a big hand for the Mistress of the Scoreboard – your very own weather girl, the lovely Brenda!'

To more jolly vamping from the Rhythm Boys, Brenda slouched onstage wearing a lurid pink evening gown. Her green bird's-nest hairdo looked as though it had been kicked into place by some couldn't-care-less eagle. Chewing, she took up her station next to the scoreboard.

'Isn't she gorgeous?' beamed Ali Pali. 'Now then. As this is our first ever Song Contest, I will briefly explain how it works. The acts will appear in alphabetical order. When all the songs have been performed, the voting will take place. The votes will be cast by twelve specially selected juries to ensure no cheating. Each jury has ten points to divide as they please, with the proviso that they are not allowed to vote for their own song. The points will be totalled by Brenda at the end.'

The audience, bored by all this mathematical talk, was beginning to doze off. But they jerked awake again as Ali raised his voice.

'And now, the big surprise of the evening – an unexpected guest! Now, I know that a lot of you were expecting our popular newsreader Sheridan Haggard to be here this evening. Sadly, he is indisposed.'

'Booo!' shouted Sheridan's disappointed fans.

'The Skeletons have withdrawn from the competition in protest,' continued Ali, 'but never mind, *we* don't care, because we have a *real* treat in store. Ladies and gentlemen, let's give a big Witchway welcome for that great star of stage and screen – *Scott Sinister*!'

Gasps, startled squeaks, and an outbreak of thunderous cheers as the popular star strolled on from the wings. As always, he wore his black velvet cape and trademark sunglasses. He waved a languid hand, acknowledging the applause. Someone threw a bunch of flowers onstage. Scott picked them up, sniffed them, then presented them to Brenda, who glamorously kicked them into the orchestra pit.

Backstage, Pongwiffy looked up smugly from the monitor. (This is a special spellovision that shows the events going on out front.)

'You see?' she said. 'I knew he'd come. Do anything for me, he will, because I'm his biggest fan.'

(In truth, Scott hadn't wanted to come, not one little bit. But he knew better than to turn down a request from Pongwiffy, who can get quite spiteful when things don't go her way. Scott knows this. He has crossed her before.)

'Scott will be awarding the fabulous prizes to tonight's winners,' announced Ali, to more cheers. Scott nodded and smiled and waved and blew kisses.

'All right, that'll do,' said Brenda. 'You can shove off now.'

Scott was happy to oblige. Live appearances were more exhausting than film work, which consists of a lot of hanging around. By simply walking onstage, he had already done more work in one evening than in the past six weeks. He hurried back to his dressing room to recover.

Back onstage, things were beginning to happen.

'And now!' Ali was shouting. 'The moment you have all been waiting for – the first song! This is the entry from the Banshees and features the Banshees' Girls' Choir singing "Oh Woe!"'

The choir trailed onstage, red-eyed and miserable-looking. There were six of them, all wearing long white nightgowns and sporting the regulation Banshee hairdo – long, wild and uncontrollably frizzy. Being professional weepers, they all carried large, businesslike handkerchiefs. The tallest – presumably the leader – raised her hanky to her nose and had a jolly good blow. This was evidently the signal to start.

> '*Oh, woe!*' wailed the Banshees. '*Oh, woe!*
> *Misery, doom and dismay,*
> *Let's all sob in our hankies,*
> *That's the Banshee way.*
> *Let's whine and wail and whinge, girls,*
> *Let's all get depressed,*
> *Let's howl and shriek for the whole of the week,*
> *Cos that's what we do best ...*'

There was quite a bit more of this sort of thing.

Banshees are good at depression. The interminable song finally ended in a welter of sobs, breast beating, hand wringing and hair tearing – and that was just the audience! The choir drooped offstage, wringing out their sodden hankies.

After a moment's pause, Ali Pali bounced back on.

'So there we have it! Thank you, ladies. A truly tragic start to the contest. And now, the Familiars, with a song entitled "Oh I Do Like to Be a Witch Familiar".'

Hugo, wearing a tiny bow tie and clutching a miniature conductor's baton, hurried onstage. He was followed by the rest of the Familiars in varying stages of stage fright. Snoop, Rory and Vernon looked boldly confident. IdentiKit and CopiCat looked smug. Speks looked unsettled, as though he would much rather be elsewhere, bringing up a pellet. Barry and Slithering Steve were both dying of shyness. Dudley brought up the rear, looking sullen. Overhead, Gaga's bats flapped about as they always did. Nobody knew what they were feeling.

Bonidle's Sloth had fallen asleep in the dressing room.

Hugo took up his position centre stage and waited until everyone had formed a relatively tidy group. There was a bit of nervous throat clearing. Rory blew the fringe out of his eyes. Then Hugo raised his baton ... and the song began.

CHAPTER TWENTY-ONE

Rescued

Sheridan Haggard sat slumped with his skull in his hands as the Thing continued to read extracts from Hugo's book by the dim light of the last, guttering candle. The funny thing was, it was a very small book and yet it never seemed to end.

'*You can lead a Hamster to its wheel but you can't make it run,*' the Thing informed him. The only response was a low moan.

'*What would we do in a world without cats, apart from be happy?*' continued the Thing. '*Even a Hamster can be big in the pictures. What do you get if you cross a cat with a skunk? Dirty looks from the skunk.*'

'Stop!' groaned Sheridan, rocking to and fro.

'*What's blue and furry? A cat holding its breath.*

Musical Hamsters fiddle with their whiskers. Cats have feelings too — but, hey, who cares? What is the best way to keep Hamsters? Don't return them. A wise Hamster ...'

'No more!' screamed Sheridan, leaping to his feet. 'I can't take any more of this rodent rubbish! Shut up, shut up, shut *up*!'

'OK,' said the Thing, sounding a bit hurt. 'Just trying to keep you amused, boss.'

'Well, don't. It's driving me out of my mind. Oh, what are we to *do*? Hours we must have been in here. Hours and hours. What time do you think it is? I've missed the midnight news, haven't I? Do you think they'll have sent out the search party yet? That candle's about to go out, isn't it? Then we'll be in the dark! I don't like it in the dark! The walls will close in and we won't see them coming! Mummeeeeeee ...'

Outside, a short way down the slope, a passing farmer on a cart clucked to his donkey, and it obediently ground to a halt. The farmer's name was Burl Bacon. The donkey was called Gervaise. Neither of them possessed a spellovision, which is why they were probably the only living creatures in the world who were neither performing in the Song Contest, watching it live nor glued to the spello.

Burl and Gervaise were currently on their way home from market, which had been cancelled owing to disinterest, although nobody had told them. Their cart was piled high with unsold baskets of eggs. It was now getting dark and they were taking the short cut home, through Goblin territory.

The reason Burl stopped was because he heard something – something that sounded suspiciously like a hollow scream, coming from a big cave set into the hill, just up the slope a bit.

'Hear that, Gervaise?' said Burl slowly, chewing on a straw reflectively. 'That there hollow screamin', comin' from behind that there boulder?'

Gervaise said nothing, because he was a donkey.

'*Heeeeeellllllp!*' came the faint cry. '*Let me ouuuut!*'

'Reckon someone's trapped in that there cave, Gervaise,' reflected Burl, nodding wisely. 'That's what oi reckons, at any rate.'

'*Arrrrgh! The walls! Heeeeeeeelllllllp!*'

'Ar,' went on Burl, agreeing with himself. 'That's what 'appened, shouldn't wonder. Shouldn't wonder if someone 'adden gone an' got theirself trapped. Now then. 'Ere's a dilemma. Shall us pay no mind an' go on back 'ome? Or shall us amble over an' take a little look?'

'*Heeeeeellllllllp! Let me ouuuuuuuuuuuut . . .*'

'Ah, sufferin' cowpats, us'll be charitable,' decided Burl. 'Righty-ho, Gervaise. In yer own time.'

Slowly, the cart creaked up the slope. When they

reached the front boulder, Gervaise clopped to a halt. Unhurriedly, Burl removed his straw hat, scratched his head, replaced his hat, cleared his throat, removed the straw from his mouth and said, ''Ello?'

'At *last*!' cried the unseen owner of the voice. Up close, it sounded rich, but wobbly. Anybody but spellovisionless Burl would have recognized it instantly, despite the wobble. 'Oh, at last you're here! Where have you *been*?'

'Oi been to market,' Burl told him, after a bit of thought. 'But it were cancelled. Ar.'

'What? You're not the search party?' wailed the voice. You could hear the hysteria bubbling away just below the surface.

'Nope,' agreed Burl. 'Don't reckon oi am.'

There came the sound of muffled voices conferring. Then, 'Did you just say you've been to market?' asked the voice.

'Ar,' agreed Burl.

'Meaning ... *it's Saturday*?'

'Ar.'

'What time on Saturday?' asked the voice, urgently.

'Eight o' the clock,' guessed Burl, looking up at the sky in wise–old–farmer fashion.

'Eight o'clock in the morning?'

'Nope. Evenin'.'

'Eight o'clock *Saturday evening*? Then it's *started*!' cried the voice, wild now. 'Whoever you are, listen carefully. My name is Sheridan Haggard. You will have heard of me. I am the famous spellovision newsreader and I have been trapped in this cave for a night and a day. I am due to present an award at a very important event, which has already started. My car has been stolen. And I will personally *mangle* whoever is responsible, I tell you that. Oh yes. I'll take him by the throat and I'll ...'

The voice, which was rising in pitch, suddenly broke off. There was a bit of mumbling. Then it resumed. It was clear that the owner was barely under control.

'Forgive me if I sound a little strange. My brain has gone missing, owing to a combination of starvation, dehydration, claustrophobia and a surfeit of rodent sayings. Just get me to a camera and I'll be fine. You will be rewarded. I can promise you that.'

Burl Bacon looked around at his baskets of unsold eggs. A reward would certainly come in handy.

'Ar. Fair enough,' he agreed, and reached for a length of rope he kept in the cart for just such an emergency as this.

It was the work of minutes – fifty of them, to be precise – to lasso the boulder, attach the other end to the cart and get Gervaise to do the donkey work. As soon as the boulder was dragged to one side, a skeletal figure came staggering out into the moonlight, supported by a short, hairy Thing.

'My oh my,' said Burl, staring at the bony one in mild surprise. 'You *'ave* been in there for a long time.'

Neither of the ex-detainees said a word. The Thing helped the trembling Skeleton to the back of the cart. Unresisting, the Skeleton climbed in and folded itself into a narrow space between the baskets of eggs. The Thing came round to the front.

'Shove over,' it ordered shortly.

'Eh?'

'I said, shove over. Got to get boss back to civilization. All right back there, boss? Relax. We'll make it yet.'

'Now, 'old your 'orses,' objected Burl. He pointed an indignant finger at Sheridan, 'He never said nothin' about needin' a lift. He said if oi got him out o' the cave oi'd get a reward. He said . . .'

The Thing jumped on to the driver's seat, snatched the reins and gave Burl a brisk shove. To his surprise and annoyance, Burl suddenly found himself sitting in a clump of thistles, watching his

165

own cart go swaying off into the distance, pulled by his own donkey.

He removed his straw hat and threw it into the dirt.

'Darn it,' said Burl. 'Ar.'

CHAPTER TWENTY-TWO
The Best Song

In Witchway Hall, the Witches sat in their dressing room watching the proceedings out front. The atmosphere was very tense. Soon, it would be their turn – and the nerves were really beginning to kick in. There was a lot of nail biting and compulsive peppermint sucking. There was nervous twiddling and fiddling with instruments. There was mass sweating and much complaining about the heat.

'My lipstick is melting,' complained Sharkadder. Tonight she was a vision in mauve. Mauve feather in mauve hair, mauve cheeks, mauve eyelids, mauve gown, mauve fingernails, mauve lipstick. She couldn't move for mauve.

On the monitor, four smarmy-looking Vampires in elegant evening dress were bowing low, having just finished a polished rendition of 'That's a Very Nice Neck, By Heck!', performed in close harmony. Their supporters were cheering loudly, but it wasn't everybody's cup of tea. A large section of the audience had shown complete indifference and talked throughout.

'Very professional,' admitted Sourmuddle. 'You've got to give credit where it's due.'

'I have reservations about the lyrics, though,' remarked Greymatter. 'Too much gore by half. Non Vampires won't go for it.'

'I must say the standard in general is higher than I expected,' admitted Sourmuddle grudgingly. 'The Mummies were good. And the Ghouls.'

'I think the Familiars are far and away the best so far,' put in Scrofula. 'They were my favourites, anyway. I was really proud of my Barry. He sang his little heart out, did you notice?'

'An' mah Rory,' added Macabre. 'Had me in tears, he did. When he sang his wee solo.' She blew her nose loudly.

'They certainly gave it their all,' agreed Sludgegooey. 'Except for Dudley, who looked rather cross, I thought.'

'Anyway,' said Ratsnappy, 'we'll certainly have our

work cut out to beat them. It was a good little song your Hugo came up with, Pongwiffy.'

'I know,' said Pongwiffy. She had mixed feelings about Hugo's song. On the one hand, she was proud that he'd written it. On the other, she could have done without the competition. 'Of course, I taught him everything he knows,' she added.

'It'll be embarrassing, though, won't it?' fretted Bendyshanks. 'If the Familiars win. Imagine. They'll get all those prizes and go on holiday. We'll never live it down. Steve'll be insufferable.'

There came a chorus of agreement. It would indeed be humiliating if the Familiars won.

On screen, it was now the turn of a lone, slightly mangy Werewolf with patched dungarees and a banjo. Sweating heavily and showing the whites of his eyes, he perched on a stool in the middle of the stage and checked his tuning. The camera zoomed in for a close-up. A bead of sweat trickled down his nose.

'Look at him,' sniffed Scrofula. 'He's going for the sympathy vote.'

'It's us next, Ag,' quivered Bagaggle.

'I know, Bag,' quavered Agglebag.

And they reached for each other's hands and squeezed them tight.

It appeared that the Werewolf had forgotten the

words to the first verse. The audience started an unsympathetic slow handclap.

There came a bang on the door and a cheap Gnome stuck its head round.

'You're next, ladies. Everybody ready?'

'We're on!' gasped Sharkadder. 'Help!'

Nobody made a move. They were all rooted to the spot with fear. Even Sourmuddle choked on her throat lozenge.

'Come on, girls,' said Pongwiffy, always good in an emergency. She picked up her guitar and marched to the door. 'Deep breaths. We know we're good. Let's blow 'em away!'

'How are you doin', boss?' called the Thing over his shoulder. They were crawling along beneath the trees at a snail's pace.

'It's uncomfortable,' complained Sheridan, rattling around miserably. 'I'm not used to this uncouth form of transport. And it's *slow*. Can't you get that animal to move any faster? We'll never get there at this rate. Oh, if only we had the *limo* ...'

At exactly that moment, something rather unexpected happened. There came a droning noise from behind, accompanied by a cloud of dust. Tyres screeched, a horn blared, there were the sounds of loud howls and demented barking – and around the bend came the limousine, with Plugugly hunched over the wheel, wearing a large pair of pink plastic comedy sunglasses with attached false moustache.

The rest of the Goblins hung on for dear life as they cornered on two wheels. Slopbucket was holding a bunch of balloons. Eyesore was wearing a Stetson. Lardo was clutching a goldfish in a plastic bag. Sproggit had a straw donkey in one hand and a stick of rock in the other. Stinkwart was wearing a beret and had a string of garlic wrapped around his neck. Hog was simultaneously eating an enormous ice cream and trying to restrain Fang the Wonder Hound, who had his head stuck out of the sunroof. Dozens of takeaway pizza boxes littered the back shelf, along with fishing rods, a set of golf clubs, a couple of tennis rackets, a large straw sombrero and a novelty ashtray inscribed *A present from Sludgehaven*.

Gervaise reared, plunged and lurched to one side as the limousine, horn still blaring, flashed by with only centimetres to spare and zoomed off into the distance. The cart's off-side wheel trembled on the verge of the ditch, then miraculously righted itself. Gervaise took a few tottery steps towards the middle of the track, then stopped, breathing heavily.

There was a pause – then Sheridan's irate skull popped up from between the egg baskets.

(Amazingly, they had all remained steady and none of the eggs was smashed.)

'My limo!' he shrieked. 'Did you see that? Goblins, driving *my limo*! *And they've got Ribsy!*' He pointed with a trembling digit. '*Follow that car!*'

CHAPTER TWENTY-THREE

More Contest

'Ladies and gentlemen, time now for the next song – "Banga Langa Bing Bong Boo!", performed by – The Singing Witches!'

Vincent Van Ghoul moved in for a tight shot as the curtain rose on the Witchway Coven, all neatly in place, looking terrified but determined to give it their best shot.

It was a very different outfit from the rowdy rabble who had turned up at Witchway Hall that first night for a bit of a singsong and a laugh. Nobody was messing about now, oh dear me no. Sourmuddle ran a tight ship. She was in this contest to *win*. She sat bolt upright at the piano, sleeves rolled up, cracking her knuckles. It was clear she meant business.

She nodded at Greymatter, who poked Bonidle with a stick. Bonidle jerked awake, caught Sourmuddle's glare and started to tap an erratic beat on the drum. Sourmuddle played an interesting little twiddly bit on the piano, followed by a series of chunky chords played over an old-fashioned honky-tonk left hand.

At this point, Gaga, the official go-go dancer, erupted from the wings and began wildly cavorting about. She had given a lot of thought to her stage costume. It consisted of yellow wellingtons and a grass hula skirt, teamed with a warm red jumper with a hole in the sleeve and a badly knitted frog on the back. A diving helmet was her chosen headgear. She looked – well, interesting.

Gradually, in response to glares from Sourmuddle, the rest of the instruments came in. Ratsnappy's reedy recorder. The twin's scratchy violins. Macabre's overwhelming bagpipes. Then the backing singers.

'*Ooby dooby doo*,' crooned Bendyshanks, Sludgegooey and Scrofula, breaking into the synchronized shuffle routine they had worked out earlier. '*Do wap, do wap!*'

It was a long introduction. Pongwiffy and Sharkadder grew visibly more tense as they waited for their big moment while Vincent ducked around them with his camera and the Tree Demon clonked

174

them on the head with his microphone. Pongwiffy looked grouchy and miserable and appeared to be threatening the Tree Demon out of the corner of her mouth. Sharkadder, in contrast, went in for ear-to-ear smiling, so they didn't match very well.

But none of this mattered when they began to sing. It didn't matter that Pongwiffy sounded like a walrus in distress or that, on occasion, Sharkadder's shrill soprano wobbled out of orbit and off into another space and time. What mattered was the *song*.

The audience loved it.

> '*Well, here's a little ditty*
> *We're sure you'll want to sing . . .*' began Pongwiffy.

In the auditorium, there was an instant stir of interest. Everyone sat up, ears pricked.

> '*It isn't very witty*
> *And it doesn't mean a thing . . .*' warbled Sharkadder.

Several people in the front row leapt to their feet and punched the air.

> '*But we know you're gonna love it,*
> *Of that we have no doubt . . .*' honked Pongwiffy.

People were clapping along in time to the rhythm now. Feet were tapping. A couple of Fiends began madly dancing in the aisle.

> '*Cos once it's lodged inside your head*
> *You'll never get it out!*' contributed Sharkadder.
> '*Ooooooooooooh . . .*' they both went, along with the backing singers. Then:
> '*Banga-langa binga-linga bonga-longa, bing, bong, boo . . .*'

And the place went mad! *This* was what the audience had come for. Oh yes. Forget the ballads and the clever stuff. What everyone wanted was a daft, jolly song with meaningless words that you could pick up in two minutes flat. Something that was easy to stomp your feet along with, or scrub your toenails to when you were lying in hot, soapy water. Something that made you feel *happy*. Something that put a soppy grin on your face. That's what they had come for. And that was exactly what they got.

There was a riot when the song finally reached its triumphant end.

'Witches! Witches!' chanted the audience, stamping their feet. 'Encore! Encore!'

'I think they liked it,' said Pongwiffy to Sharkadder out of the corner of her mouth.

'I think they did,' agreed Sharkadder, grinning and bowing low.

'More!' raved the audience. 'More! More! More!'

They weren't allowed more, though. One go at your song, that's all you got. To loud boos, Ali Pali hurried onstage, signalled for the curtain to be brought down, then began to explain the rules yet again. This was a contest. Each act performed the song once, and once only. There were still two acts to go – the Wizards and the Zombies. Then, and only then, could the specially selected juries cast their votes. So if the Witches could kindly get offstage and everyone could take their seats again, perhaps things could move on. At this point, a cheap Gnome scuttled onstage and whispered in his ear.

'Correction,' amended Ali, speaking directly to camera. 'There is only one more act. The Zombies have withdrawn because they've all got sore throats.'

'Sore at losing, more like!' heckled Pongwiffy, from behind the curtain. Zombie supporters in the audience blushed and hung their heads. They knew it was true.

The Wizards, however, were made of sterner stuff. Under the leadership of Dave the Druid, they had worked hard on their song. There was no way they would step back and let the Witches win without a fight. 'The Long and Winding Beard' would be given an airing, like it or not. (Ronald, of course, was particularly keen, because he had written the words.)

Wisely, the Wizards didn't bother with instruments. Their strength was in song. They concentrated on the vocals. Dave the Druid had done a good job. He had set Ronald's words to music. Over the past two weeks, he had made the Wizards struggle out of their armchairs and practise scales and do breathing exercises. He had taken them walking and stopped them eating too many sausages. He had divided everyone up into basses and tenors and falsettos and explained all about harmony. He had worked on pitch, tone and timing. He was a stickler for diction too. Every word was crisp and clear. End consonants were particularly emphasized.

'*The longga andda windingg beardda,*' sang the Wizards.
'*Is alwayss in the jammm,*
It'ss often fullll of toastttt
And egggg and bitss of hammmm.
I'll never shave it offf,
For that's the way I ammmmm …'

The Witches stood in the wings, listening.

'They're *quite* good,' decided Sourmuddle, adding mysteriously, 'though I've never been one for male-voice choirs since I got bitten by one.'

'They're very good, actually,' sighed Sharkadder. 'Ronald wrote the words, you know. Talent runs in our family, as well as beauty.'

'They're not a patch on us, though,' said Pongwiffy, oozing confidence, now her bit was all over. 'We'll win. I'll bet my wand on it.'

'I'm not so sure,' fretted Sharkadder.

'Beyond any shadow of doubt,' said Pongwiffy firmly. She hugged her guitar. 'A song like that? And talent like ours? No question.'

At this point, let's just pop back and see how the car chase is coming along.

Dramatic incidents don't happen much in the life of a cart-pulling donkey, and Gervaise had decided to get into the spirit of things. Right now, he was galloping after the limo at an alarming rate, with the Thing fighting to hang on to the reins. Sheridan Haggard was poised precariously on the swaying cart, a basket of eggs in each hand.

'Wot's 'appenin'?' bellowed Plugugly, wrenching the steering wheel hard left and missing the ditch by half an air molecule. 'Who's dat chasin' us?'

They zoomed round a corner and past a holly tree. All Slopbucket's balloons burst in a flurry of sharp pops. Fang the Wonder Hound was barking crazily and attempting to wriggle out through the sunroof. Several twigs and low-lying branches were lodged in his rib cage. The wind whistled through his bones.

'I can't see!' screeched Eyesore. 'There's egg all over the back window!'

'Oh no!' wailed Sproggit. 'Flyin' chickens!'

'That ain't no chickens!' bawled Hog. 'It's that Skellington! 'E wants 'is dog back! 'E's throwin' eggs at us!'

'Give 'im the dog!' screeched Stinkwart. 'Push it out the sunroof!'

'Don't you dare!' warned Plugugly, letting go of the steering wheel and shaking his fist. 'You leave Fang alone, you – you *wicked* Goblin!'

'Log pile comin' up!' screamed Eyesore, covering his eyes. 'Plug! Watch the road!'

Plugugly swivelled round and grabbed the wheel. The car lunged to one side. More eggs splattered the windscreen.

'Watch out!'

'Arrrrgggh!'

'Faster, Plug! Go faster!'

Oh yes. Coming along nicely.

CHAPTER TWENTY-FOUR

And The Winner Is...

At Witchway Hall, the votes were beginning to come in. Backstage, dressing rooms fell silent. Trembling contestants clustered around the monitors or hid in corners with their hands over their faces.

Only Scott Sinister was uninterested in the whole business. The monitor in his private dressing room was on, but he wasn't even watching. Bored out of his mind, he reclined on a couch with chunks of cucumber balanced on his eyelids, dreaming of the moment he could hand over the trophy, make his excuses, hopefully avoid that awful Pongwiffy and hurry off back to his rich and famous lifestyle.

Out front, Vince's camera was trained steadily on Ali Pali, who stood next to the scoreboard armed with earphones and a clipboard. Brenda, clearly underwhelmed by the whole thing, was reading a magazine.

'Yes, folks, I've just heard that we're now ready to hear the votes of the Troll jury,' announced Ali. He raised his head and addressed the air. 'Hello, Trolls, are you there?'

After a worrying moment or two, the air rang with a loud fit of coughing. Then a gruff, disembodied voice with an odd echo, which made it sound like it was coming from under a mountain (which it probably was), replied, 'Yer, Ali, 'ere we are.'

The Tree Demon held up a board saying *CLAP*. Obediently, the audience clapped.

''Ere are the votes of the Trollish jury,' the voice went on. 'The Banshees – nuthin'. Too depressin'.'

'Banshees – no points,' Ali solemnly relayed to Brenda, who popped a bubble and slotted a big zero into the scoreboard.

Backstage, the heartbroken Banshees howled and wrung their nighties.

'Familiars – not bad at all. Good solo from the Haggis. Three,' continued the Trollish voice. Faint cheers could be heard coming from the Familiars' dressing room.

'Familiars – three points,' Ali told Brenda, pointlessly.

'Ghosts – quite effective. Two.'

'Ghosts, two points.'

'Ghouls – borin'. One.'

'Ghouls – one point,' interpreted Ali.

'Gnomes – four. Quite appealin' we thought that was.'

'Gnomes – four points.'

'It's taking forever,' complained Pongwiffy, never known for her patience. 'Can't they speed it up a bit? Just give us the trophy, take our photograph with Scott, let us sing our song again and eat any celebration cake that's going, then go home. We're off to sunny Sludgehaven tomorrow, and Hugo and I haven't even packed yet. That's if I decide to take him. I still haven't really forgiven him for entering the contest without permission.'

'Shhh,' hissed everyone. More points were being awarded. In fact, they were coming in thick and fast now. Ali and Brenda were finding it hard to keep up. Moreover, they were becoming increasingly odd.

'Mummies – seven,' intoned the Troll voice. 'Vampires – thirteen. Werewolf – twenty-three. Witches – eighty-five.'

'Yesssssss!' went up the excited cry from the Witches, and Gaga did a celebratory pirouette.

'I'm sorry, I'll have to stop you there,' Ali told the air, sternly. 'That is more than ten points.'

'What?' said the disembodied voice.

'Ten points,' explained Ali, wearily. 'Each jury gets *ten points,* remember? I've been through it a million times. I thought we were all clear.'

At this, there was a bit of invisible whispering, if there is such a thing. Then, 'We're Trolls,' said the voice. 'We'll have as many points as we likes. We liked the Witches' song. It's catchy. We *wants* to give it eighty-five. And we liked the Wizards' song as well, though not quite as much. So we give that eighty-two and a half.'

Backstage, a loud '*hoorah!*' came from the Wizards' dressing room.

'You can't do that,' argued Ali. 'There have to be rules.'

'Yeah, well, we've just changed 'em,' the disembodied voice informed him. 'We don't like your poncey scoring system. We want more points.'

'It's too complicated,' snapped Ali.

'No it ain't. A hundred an' fifty's a good top mark, not too big, not too small. While we're about it, we'll upgrade the Familiars to twenty-seven and a half, just because we're Trolls and we can. An' finally, we gives the talented Troll group Cliff and the Chips the top mark of *one hundred an' fifty.* That concludes the votes of the Trollish jury. Wanna make somethin' of it?'

'You see?' Sourmuddle scolded Pongwiffy. 'You shouldn't count your chickens. The Wizards have got nearly the same as us.'

'How many more juries to go?' asked Sharkadder, who had gone sweaty with nerves. Streaks of mauve make-up trickled down her flushed cheeks.

'Twelve.'

'Well, I can't watch any more. I'm going to lie down. Tell me when it's over.'

Meanwhile, back with the Goblins, the eggs were coming thick and fast. They came whistling overhead from behind, falling in an arc and bursting open on the windscreen in runny yellow splats. Plugugly stabbed blindly at a button on the dashboard in a desperate attempt to activate the wipers. The heater came on and the eggs began to scramble.

'I can't see!' bawled Plugugly, wrenching the steering wheel. 'How close are dey? I can't see! I can't – *Ow!*'

Everyone gasped, jerked upright and bit their tongues as they went down a pothole. Sproggit's stick of rock went up his nose.

'I dunno how close, do I?' cried Eyesore. 'I keep *tellin'* you, I can't see!'

'Well, stand up an' look out de sunroof! Hold on, goin' right!'

Tyres screamed as the limo swerved hard to the left.

'Ooooooh!' wailed the Goblins, in chorus.

'Slow down, Plug!' begged Slopbucket. 'We don't want to be on this road. We can shake 'em off if we get on the back roads.'

This was an amazingly sensible suggestion, for a Goblin. Slopbucket came up with it by accident, probably because his brains were being shaken up. It is a great pity that nobody took any notice.

'Faster!' shrieked Sproggit, gnawing the stuffing out of his straw donkey. 'Fasterfasterfaster! Ya-hoooo!'

'Which shall I do?' screamed Plugugly. 'Go fast or go slow?'

Nobody heard. They were all howling too loudly. They had seen something in front: the silhouette of a large, familiar building. It was still some way off in the distance – but it was coming ever closer.

'Oh well,' said Plugugly with a shrug. 'I'll do bofe!'

And the limousine went into a wild spin as he pressed both pedals at the same time.

In Witchway Hall, things were balanced on a knife edge. The Troll jury's refusal to conform had set the tone for the rest of the juries who, to Ali's rising despair, ran roughshod over the rules and awarded haphazard points to whoever they liked. The scoreboard was now bizarre in the extreme. It said:

Banshees	0
Familiars	197½
Ghosts	152
Ghouls	151
Gnomes	158
Mummies	179
Trolls	150
Vampires	188
Werewolf	156
Witches	199
Wizards	199

Imagine the tension. Twelve of the thirteen juries had now voted. With one exception, they had all given their own song top marks. All except the Banshee jury, who awarded 'Oh Woe!' zero points because they liked to make themselves miserable.

It was now the turn of the Mummy jury. Out of respect for their great age and the fact that most of them had royal connections, they had been left until last.

Ali Pali, annoyed that he had lost control of the scoring, but determined to see things through to the bitter end, strode to the centre of the stage and addressed the audience.

'And now, ladies and gentlemen and viewers at home, it's time for the votes from our final jury tonight. Coming live from a pyramid in Egypt –' Ali paused to fiddle with his headphones – 'sorry, I stand corrected, yes, sorry, *dead* from a pyramid in Egypt, we welcome the Mummy jury. Hello? Hello? Is that the Mummies? Mummies, are you there?'

'Good evening, Ali,' creaked a dry, ancient voice. It reminded you of sand and wind and embalming fluid. 'This is King Psioriasis the Third, spokesman for the Mummy jury. Viewers at home, greetings. Before we give you our votes, we would like to make a comment. In our ancient wisdom, we feel we must point out that the original scoring system was much fairer than the one introduced by the Trollish jury, which is, quite frankly, ludicrous.'

'Hear hear,' agreed Ali. 'That's just what I said. Thank you, sire. At last, someone with sense. A round of applause for King Psioriasis the Third, ladies and gentlemen.'

'Never mind all that,' continued the dry voice, somewhat testily. 'Let's just get on, shall we? In the interests of ancient justice, we shall revert to the first system. So, with no more ado, here are the results of the Mummy jury. Banshees – no points. Familiars – three points . . .'

'Oh no!' groaned Pongwiffy, backstage. 'One hundred and ninety-seven and a half plus three. That makes – um – how much does that make?'

'Two hundred and a half points,' said Greymatter grimly. 'That takes them higher than us. If we get zero, we're done for!'

At this, several Witches fainted. Nobody noticed, so they sheepishly came to again and joined the tense crowd round the monitor.

In his dressing room, Scott Sinister gave a little sigh, removed the chunks of cucumber from his eyes and reached for the trophy. Any minute now, he'd be on.

'Ghosts – zero,' went on the dry voice out front. 'Ghouls – zero. Gnomes – one point. Mummies – well, much as we would like to, we cannot vote for our own. Very well done, though, Xotindis and Xstufitu, you did us proud. Trolls – zero. Vampires – two points. Werewolf – one point.'

There was an excited buzz. The moment everyone was waiting for had arrived.

'That leaves three points,' continued the dry voice. 'We could have awarded one and a half each to the Witches and the Wizards, which would have resulted in an unsatisfactory tie. So, in our ancient

189

wisdom, we have decided to award all three points to ...'

You really don't need to be told what happens next, do you? You've seen it coming.

There came the sound of squealing brakes and a screaming engine, mixed in with howling voices – and, to everyone's horror, a large section of the right-hand wall of the auditorium imploded under the impact of a large, black, smoking, egg-splattered monster, which, in another life, had once been a gleaming limousine. Bricks and plaster sprayed down upon the audience as the ruined car tore across the hall, missing the front row of the stalls by a whisker. With a loud crump, it embedded itself in the opposite wall.

That caused plenty of commotion in itself.

Things got even crazier when the passenger door fell off and a Gaggle of howling Goblins poured out, like dirty water from an unblocked pipe.

At this point, the cart arrived through the hole in the wall, adding a wild-eyed donkey, a dishevelled Thing, a Skeleton with a grudge and a lot of eggs to the already volatile mixture.

Loads of things happened then. Dressing-room doors crashed open and the various contestants came rushing out and made for the stage.

Pongwiffy spotted the Goblins.

Fang the Wonder Hound spotted Dudley.

Age-old enemies suddenly spotted each other and decided to break whatever wobbly truce was currently in place. All those eggs around, shame to miss the opportunity.

Ali Pali was running about in circles, trying to regain a semblance of control – but it was a losing battle. Brenda tucked up her pink evening dress and waded in amongst it all, seizing cheap Gnomes and glamorously banging their heads together.

Through it all, Vincent Van Ghoul continued to film, while the Tree Demon ran here and there with his microphone, capturing the whole shocking thing on tape. Manfully, the Witchway Rhythm Boys played on.

We won't dwell on the fight between Sheridan Haggard and Scott Sinister, which happened much later on. Something about non-payment of castle rent. The Thing tried to break it up, but failed.

We don't want to hear how everything got too much for poor Sharkadder, who came over all emotional and cried, then stamped her foot and blamed Pongwiffy.

Neither do we want to know what a spectacle Brenda made of herself. Or what Fang the Wonder Hound did to Dudley, aided and abetted by Hugo. Or how the Witches and the Wizards got into a slanging match, which ended in them going outside and having a Magical showdown, which ended in Witchway Hall burning down.

We *really* don't want to know what Pongwiffy did to the Goblins. It's too disgraceful and would make a very unpleasant ending to the whole sorry affair. Suffice to say, it did for her guitar.

The fact remains that it happened, and everybody involved later felt rather ashamed of themselves and just looked sheepish when they passed each other in the woods.

And what did the viewers at home make of all this?

They disapproved, of course. All that mess and mayhem and not even a clear result.

But they all agreed it was great spellovision.

CHAPTER TWENTY-FIVE

The End

'Moon's up. I think I'll go out,' said Pongwiffy to Hugo, a day or two later.

They had just finished supper. Hugo had cooked a really nice pie. Through the broken window, the moon sailed high and the stars were coming out. Pongwiffy had her feet on her plate and was picking at her nails with a fork. Hugo was doing the crossword puzzle, which was back in the *Daily Miracle* by popular demand.

It was a cosy scene. Everything had settled back to normal. Pongwiffy had made the Goblins return every last bit of rubbish, so the dump was restored to its former glory. In fact, it was even better than before, being now full of dumped spellovisions.

Nobody was interested any more. Like most new fads, it had burnt itself out.

Fang the Wonder Hound, now known as Ribs again, was back with Sheridan, who had moved out of Sinister Towers and was said to be writing a book now that his job as newsreader was no more. (However, it must be said that Ribs sometimes goes missing in order to visit his old friend Plugugly, who is always thrilled to see him.)

'So vhere you go?' asked Hugo.

'I thought I'd pop out and get rid of the guitar.'

'Jah?' Hugo was surprised. 'I thought you say it antique? Zat maybe it belong to zat old Rasperry man?'

'Yes, well, maybe, who cares. I keep tripping over it. And there's only one string left and the neck's gone all unstuck again.'

'Oh, right,' nodded Hugo. 'No more music, zen?'

'No. I'm bored with music now. It was fun for a while. But I think I've probably gone as far as I can with my guitar playing. Which is – well, if I'm being honest, nowhere, really.'

There was a longish pause while Hugo just sat tight.

'You're supposed to say, *Oh no, Mistress,*' Pongwiffy reminded him. 'That's what you're *supposed* to say.'

'*A vise Hamster knows ven to keep his mouth shut*,' quoted Hugo.

There was another longish pause. Then they caught each other's eye and burst into laughter.

'You're right,' said Pongwiffy, wiping her eyes and blowing her nose on the tablecloth. 'I wasn't very good, was I? Come on, pardner. What say we both go out and dump the guitar.'

So that's what they did. It arced over the rubbish dump and fell on the far side with a *plink*.

'Good riddance,' said Pongwiffy, dusting her hands. 'Let's get the cauldron out and do some Magic, eh? What do you say?'

'Yep!' agreed Hugo. And together they went back into the hovel.

On the far side of the tip, an old tramp happened to be passing by. The broken guitar fell at his feet.

'Well, durn me,' said a low, rasping voice. 'If that don't beat all. Whoever woulda believed it? After all these years.'

And Wild Raspberry Johnson bent down, picked it up and wandered slowly on.

Hugo's favourite sayings from

The Little Book of Hamster Wit and Wisdom

Hamsters are better than cats.

Blue are the violets,
Red are the roses.
Hamsters are furry,
With little pink noses.

What kind of hamsters live at the North Pole?
Cold ones.

What's blue and furry?
A cat holding its breath.

Musical hamsters fiddle with their whiskers.

Cats have feelings too – but, hey, who cares?

A wise hamster knows when to keep his mouth shut.